when speaks the dragon!

Writer: STAN LEE
Penciler: JACK KIRBY

Inker: VINCE COLLETTA
Colorist: MATT MILLA
Letterers: ART SIMEK & SAM ROSEN

Cover Artists: OLIVIER COIPEL, MARK MORALES
& LAURA MARTIN

Collection Editors: MARK D. BEAZLEY & CORY LEVINE
Assistant Editors: ALEX STARBUCK & NELSON RIBEIRO
Editor, Special Projects: JENNIFER GRÜNWALD
Senior Editor, Special Projects: JEFF YOUNGQUIST
SVP of Print & Digital Publishing Sales: DAVID GABRIEL
Research: JEPH YORK & DANA PERKINS
Select Art Reconstruction: TOM ZIUKO
Production: JERRON QUALITY COLOR & JOE FRONTIRRE
Book Designer: SPRING HOTELING

Editor In Chief: AXEL ALONSO
Chief Creative Officer: JOE QUESADA
Publisher: DAN BUCKLEY
Executive Producer: ALAN FINE

SPECIAL THANKS TO RALPH MACCHIO

Visit us at www.abdopublishing.com

Reinforced library bound editions published in 2014 by Spotlight, a division of the ABDO Group, PO Box 398166, Minneapolis, MN 55439. Spotlight produces high-quality reinforced library bound editions for schools and libraries. Published by agreement with Marvel Characters, Inc.

Printed in the United States of America, North Mankato, Minnesota.
042013
092013
This book contains at least 10% recycled material.

Library of Congress Cataloging-in-Publication Data

Lee, Stan.
When speaks the dragon! / story by Stan Lee ; art by Jack Kirby.
pages cm. -- (Thor, tales of Asgard)
"Marvel."
Summary: An adaptation, in graphic novel form, of comic books revealing the adventures of the Norse Gods and Thor before he came to Earth, featuring the godling's visit to Nastrond, where an ancient evil lurks.
ISBN 978-1-61479-174-4 (alk. paper)
1. Thor (Norse deity)--Juvenile fiction. 2. Graphic novels. [1. Graphic novels. 2. Thor (Norse deity)--Fiction. 3. Mythology, Norse--Fiction.] I. Kirby, Jack, illustrator. II. Title.
PZ7.S81712Whe 2013
741.5'973--dc23

2013005408

Spotlight

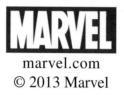

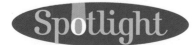

All Spotlight books are reinforced library bindings and manufactured in the United States of America.

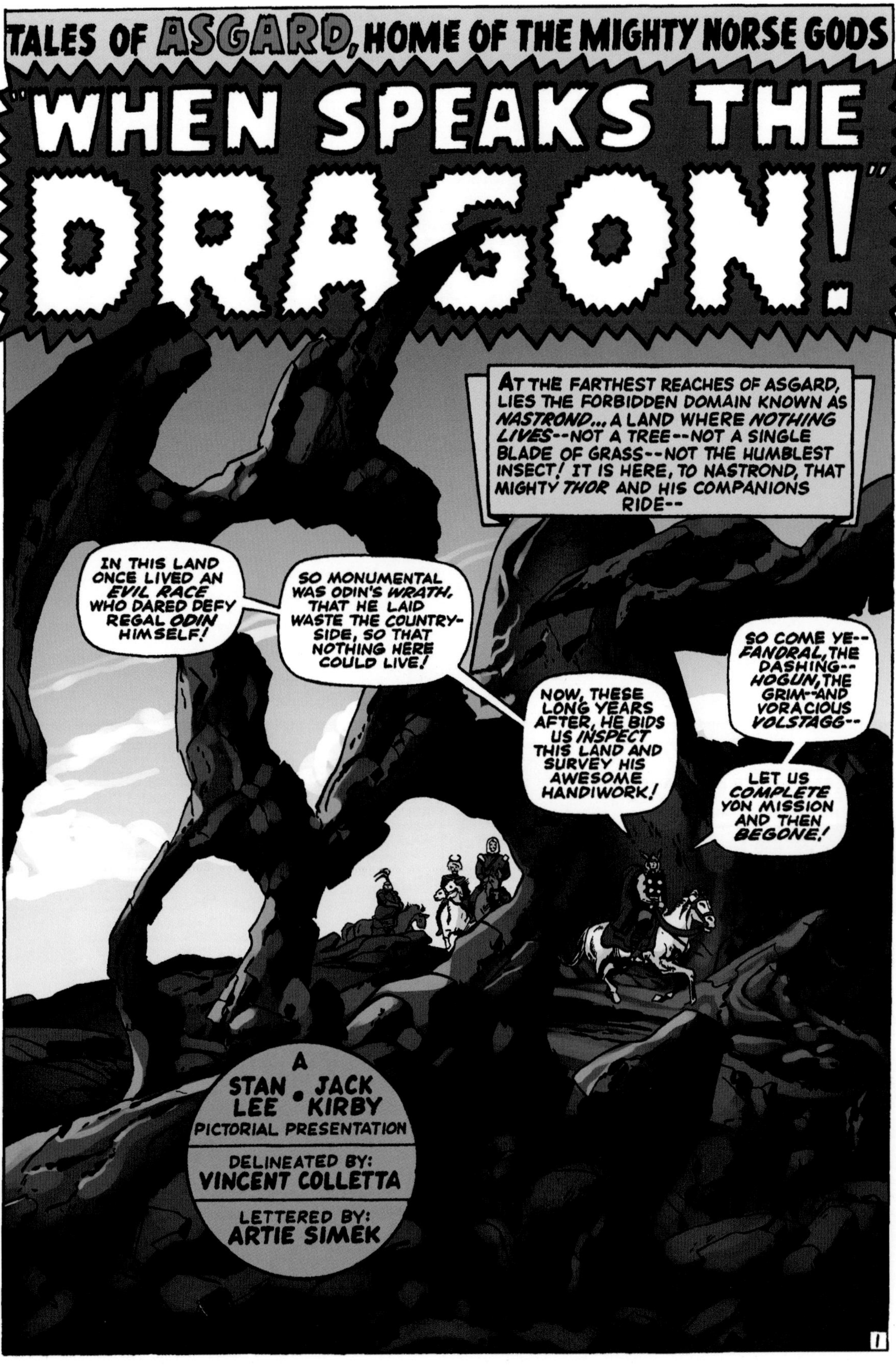
TALES OF ASGARD, HOME OF THE MIGHTY NORSE GODS
"WHEN SPEAKS THE DRAGON!"
AT THE FARTHEST REACHES OF ASGARD, LIES THE FORBIDDEN DOMAIN KNOWN AS NASTROND... A LAND WHERE NOTHING LIVES--NOT A TREE--NOT A SINGLE BLADE OF GRASS--NOT THE HUMBLEST INSECT! IT IS HERE, TO NASTROND, THAT MIGHTY THOR AND HIS COMPANIONS RIDE--
IN THIS LAND ONCE LIVED AN EVIL RACE WHO DARED DEFY REGAL ODIN HIMSELF!
SO MONUMENTAL WAS ODIN'S WRATH, THAT HE LAID WASTE THE COUNTRY-SIDE, SO THAT NOTHING HERE COULD LIVE!
NOW, THESE LONG YEARS AFTER, HE BIDS US INSPECT THIS LAND AND SURVEY HIS AWESOME HANDIWORK!
SO COME YE--FANDRAL, THE DASHING--HOGUN, THE GRIM--AND VORACIOUS VOLSTAGG--
LET US COMPLETE YON MISSION AND THEN BEGONE!
A STAN LEE • JACK KIRBY PICTORIAL PRESENTATION
DELINEATED BY: VINCENT COLLETTA
LETTERED BY: ARTIE SIMEK
1

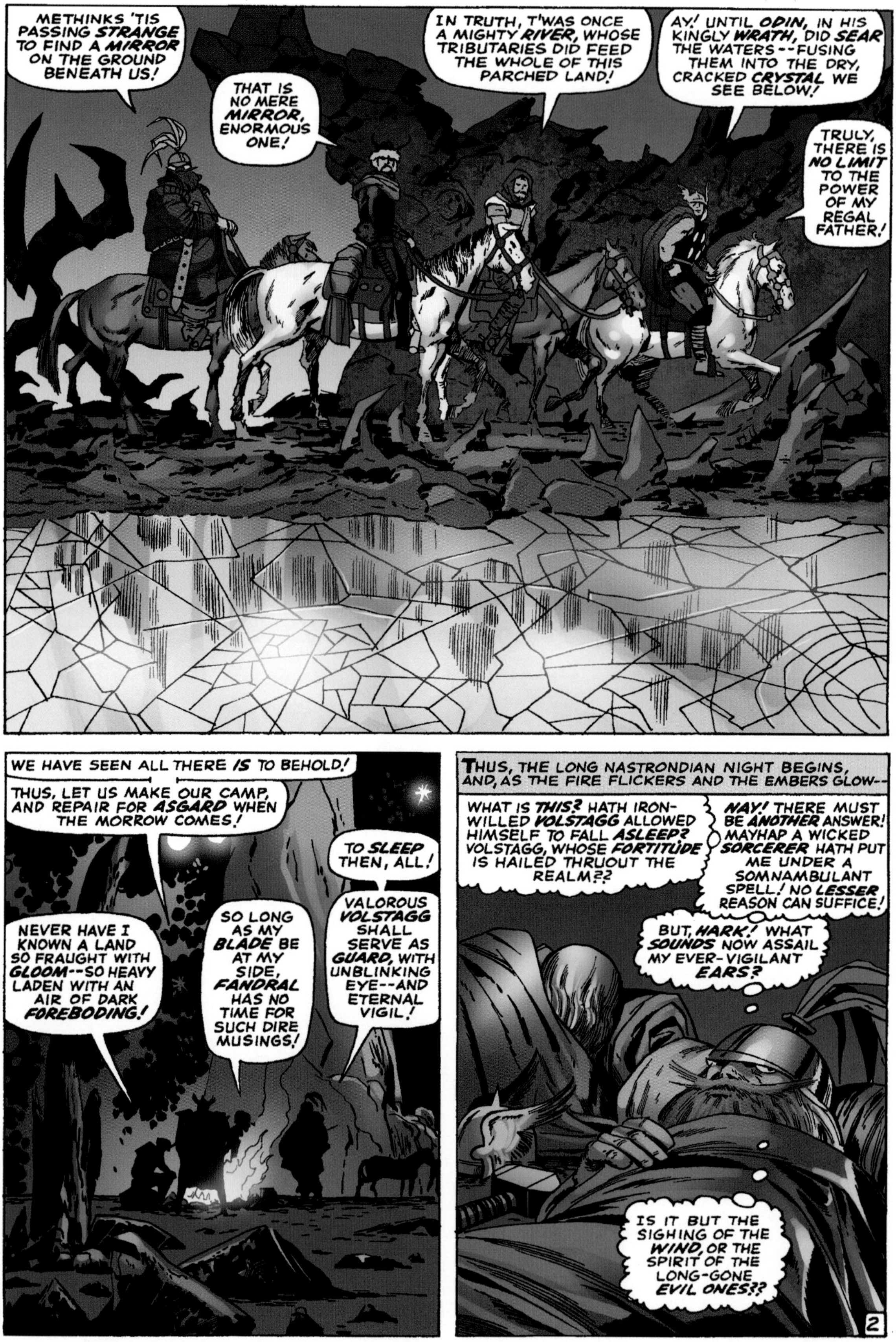
METHINKS 'TIS PASSING STRANGE TO FIND A MIRROR ON THE GROUND BENEATH US!
THAT IS NO MERE MIRROR, ENORMOUS ONE!
IN TRUTH, T'WAS ONCE A MIGHTY RIVER, WHOSE TRIBUTARIES DID FEED THE WHOLE OF THIS PARCHED LAND!
AY! UNTIL ODIN, IN HIS KINGLY WRATH, DID SEAR THE WATERS--FUSING THEM INTO THE DRY, CRACKED CRYSTAL WE SEE BELOW!
TRULY, THERE IS NO LIMIT TO THE POWER OF MY REGAL FATHER!
WE HAVE SEEN ALL THERE IS TO BEHOLD!
THUS, LET US MAKE OUR CAMP, AND REPAIR FOR ASGARD WHEN THE MORROW COMES!
TO SLEEP THEN, ALL!
NEVER HAVE I KNOWN A LAND SO FRAUGHT WITH GLOOM--SO HEAVY LADEN WITH AN AIR OF DARK FOREBODING!
SO LONG AS MY BLADE BE AT MY SIDE, FANDRAL HAS NO TIME FOR SUCH DIRE MUSINGS!
VALOROUS VOLSTAGG SHALL SERVE AS GUARD, WITH UNBLINKING EYE--AND ETERNAL VIGIL!
THUS, THE LONG NASTRONDIAN NIGHT BEGINS, AND, AS THE FIRE FLICKERS AND THE EMBERS GLOW--
WHAT IS THIS? HATH IRON-WILLED VOLSTAGG ALLOWED HIMSELF TO FALL ASLEEP? VOLSTAGG, WHOSE FORTITUDE IS HAILED THRUOUT THE REALM??
NAY! THERE MUST BE ANOTHER ANSWER! MAYHAP A WICKED SORCERER HATH PUT ME UNDER A SOMNAMBULANT SPELL! NO LESSER REASON CAN SUFFICE!
BUT, HARK! WHAT SOUNDS NOW ASSAIL MY EVER-VIGILANT EARS?
IS IT BUT THE SIGHING OF THE WIND, OR THE SPIRIT OF THE LONG-GONE EVIL ONES??
2

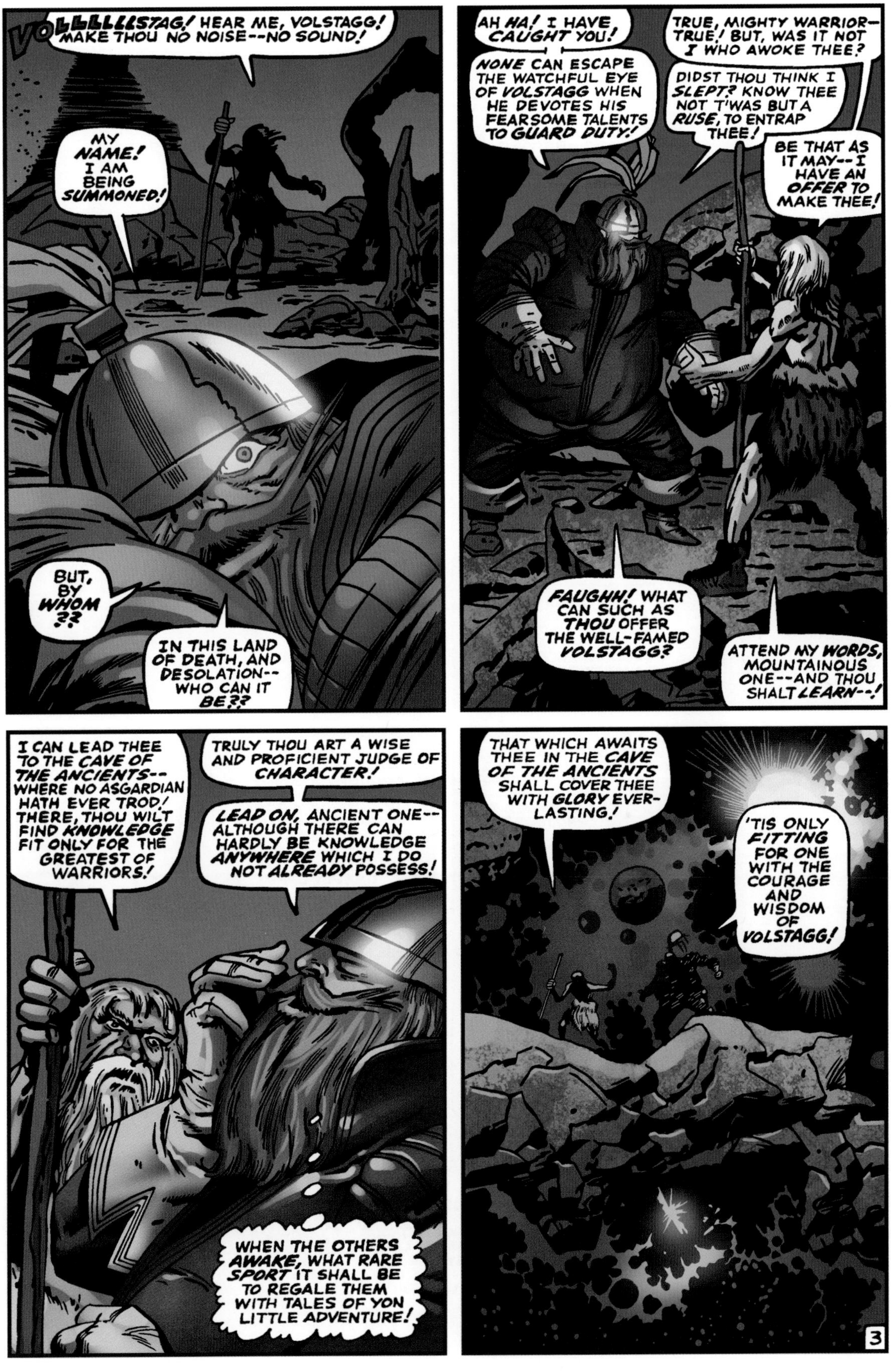
VOLLLLLLSTAG! HEAR ME, VOLSTAGG! MAKE THOU NO NOISE--NO SOUND!
MY NAME! I AM BEING SUMMONED!
BUT, BY WHOM ??
IN THIS LAND OF DEATH, AND DESOLATION-- WHO CAN IT BE??
AH HA! I HAVE CAUGHT YOU!
NONE CAN ESCAPE THE WATCHFUL EYE OF VOLSTAGG WHEN HE DEVOTES HIS FEARSOME TALENTS TO GUARD DUTY!
TRUE, MIGHTY WARRIOR-- TRUE! BUT, WAS IT NOT I WHO AWOKE THEE?
DIDST THOU THINK I SLEPT? KNOW THEE NOT T'WAS BUT A RUSE, TO ENTRAP THEE!
BE THAT AS IT MAY-- I HAVE AN OFFER TO MAKE THEE!
FAUGHH! WHAT CAN SUCH AS THOU OFFER THE WELL-FAMED VOLSTAGG?
ATTEND MY WORDS, MOUNTAINOUS ONE--AND THOU SHALT LEARN--!
I CAN LEAD THEE TO THE CAVE OF THE ANCIENTS-- WHERE NO ASGARDIAN HATH EVER TROD! THERE, THOU WILT FIND KNOWLEDGE FIT ONLY FOR THE GREATEST OF WARRIORS!
TRULY THOU ART A WISE AND PROFICIENT JUDGE OF CHARACTER!
LEAD ON, ANCIENT ONE-- ALTHOUGH THERE CAN HARDLY BE KNOWLEDGE ANYWHERE WHICH I DO NOT ALREADY POSSESS!
WHEN THE OTHERS AWAKE, WHAT RARE SPORT IT SHALL BE TO REGALE THEM WITH TALES OF YON LITTLE ADVENTURE!
THAT WHICH AWAITS THEE IN THE CAVE OF THE ANCIENTS SHALL COVER THEE WITH GLORY EVER-LASTING!
'TIS ONLY FITTING FOR ONE WITH THE COURAGE AND WISDOM OF VOLSTAGG!
3

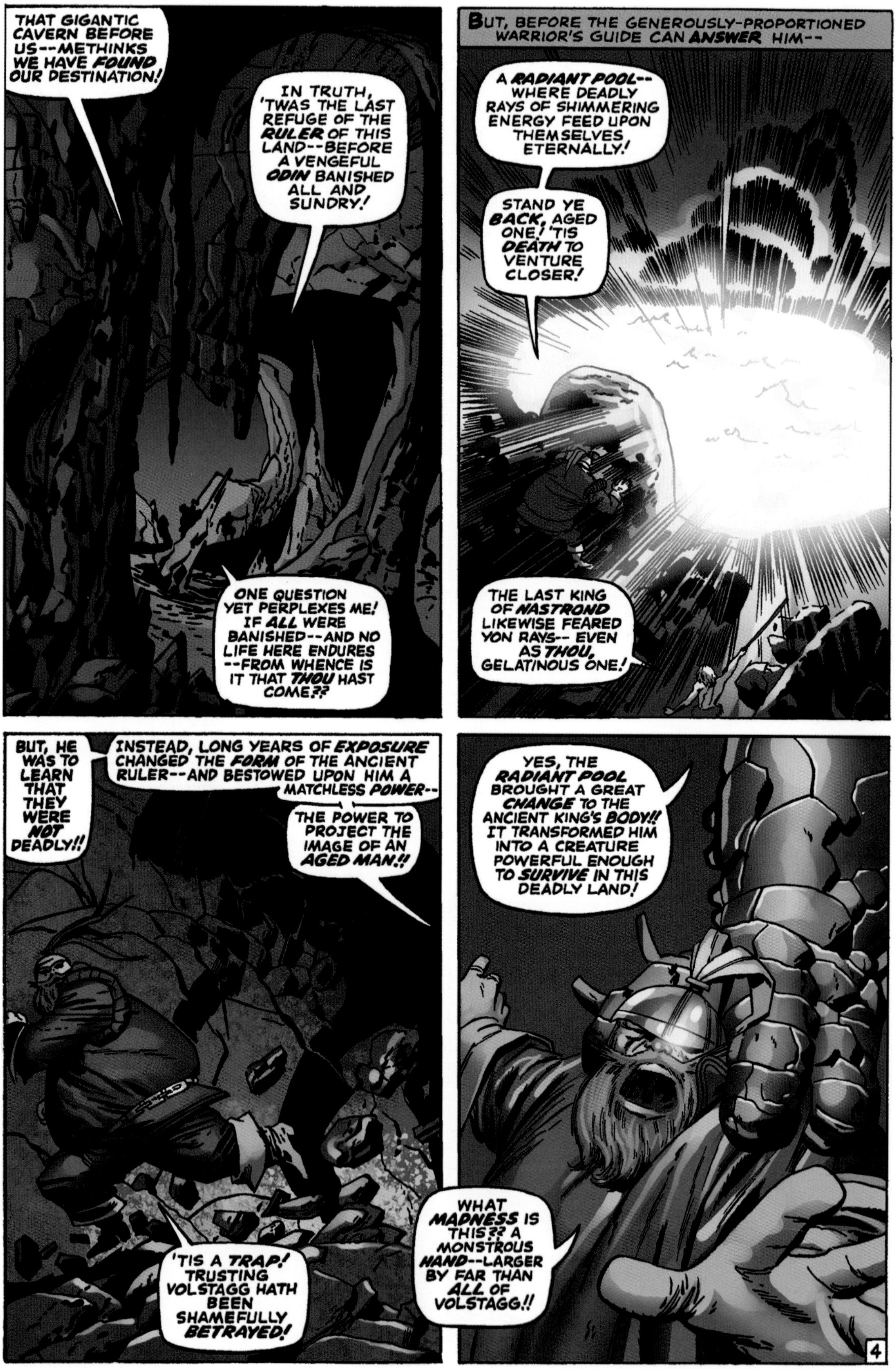
THAT GIGANTIC CAVERN BEFORE US--METHINKS WE HAVE FOUND OUR DESTINATION!
IN TRUTH, 'TWAS THE LAST REFUGE OF THE RULER OF THIS LAND--BEFORE A VENGEFUL ODIN BANISHED ALL AND SUNDRY!
ONE QUESTION YET PERPLEXES ME! IF ALL WERE BANISHED--AND NO LIFE HERE ENDURES --FROM WHENCE IS IT THAT THOU HAST COME??
BUT, BEFORE THE GENEROUSLY-PROPORTIONED WARRIOR'S GUIDE CAN ANSWER HIM--
A RADIANT POOL--WHERE DEADLY RAYS OF SHIMMERING ENERGY FEED UPON THEMSELVES ETERNALLY!
STAND YE BACK, AGED ONE! 'TIS DEATH TO VENTURE CLOSER!
THE LAST KING OF NASTROND LIKEWISE FEARED YON RAYS-- EVEN AS THOU, GELATINOUS ONE!
BUT, HE WAS TO LEARN THAT THEY WERE NOT DEADLY!!
INSTEAD, LONG YEARS OF EXPOSURE CHANGED THE FORM OF THE ANCIENT RULER--AND BESTOWED UPON HIM A MATCHLESS POWER--
THE POWER TO PROJECT THE IMAGE OF AN AGED MAN!!
'TIS A TRAP! TRUSTING VOLSTAGG HATH BEEN SHAMEFULLY BETRAYED!
YES, THE RADIANT POOL BROUGHT A GREAT CHANGE TO THE ANCIENT KING'S BODY!! IT TRANSFORMED HIM INTO A CREATURE POWERFUL ENOUGH TO SURVIVE IN THIS DEADLY LAND!
WHAT MADNESS IS THIS?? A MONSTROUS HAND--LARGER BY FAR THAN ALL OF VOLSTAGG!!
4

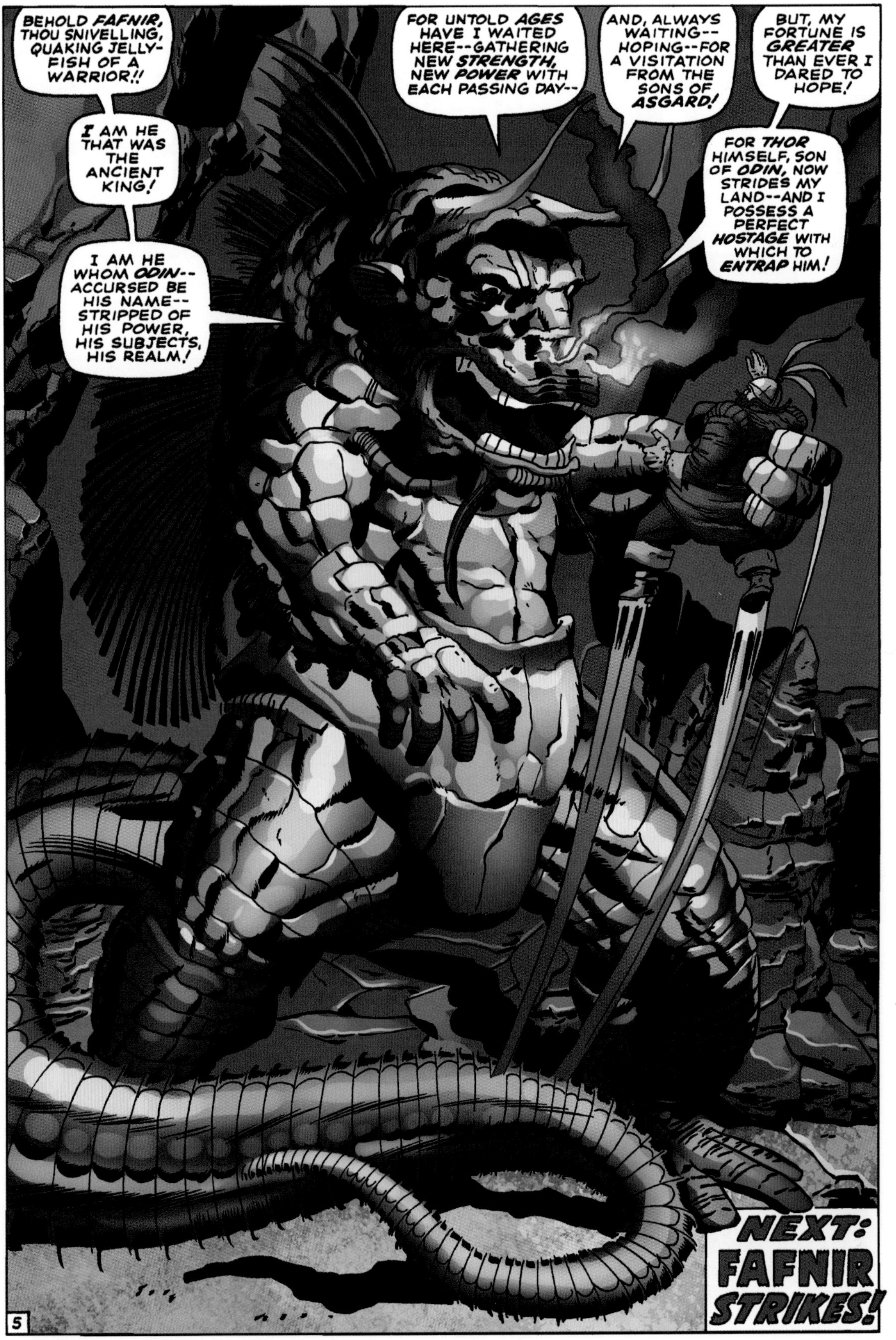
BEHOLD FAFNIR, THOU SNIVELLING, QUAKING JELLY-FISH OF A WARRIOR!!
I AM HE THAT WAS THE ANCIENT KING!
I AM HE WHOM ODIN--ACCURSED BE HIS NAME--STRIPPED OF HIS POWER, HIS SUBJECTS, HIS REALM!
FOR UNTOLD AGES HAVE I WAITED HERE--GATHERING NEW STRENGTH, NEW POWER WITH EACH PASSING DAY--
AND, ALWAYS WAITING--HOPING--FOR A VISITATION FROM THE SONS OF ASGARD!
BUT, MY FORTUNE IS GREATER THAN EVER I DARED TO HOPE!
FOR THOR HIMSELF, SON OF ODIN, NOW STRIDES MY LAND--AND I POSSESS A PERFECT HOSTAGE WITH WHICH TO ENTRAP HIM!
NEXT: FAFNIR STRIKES!
5

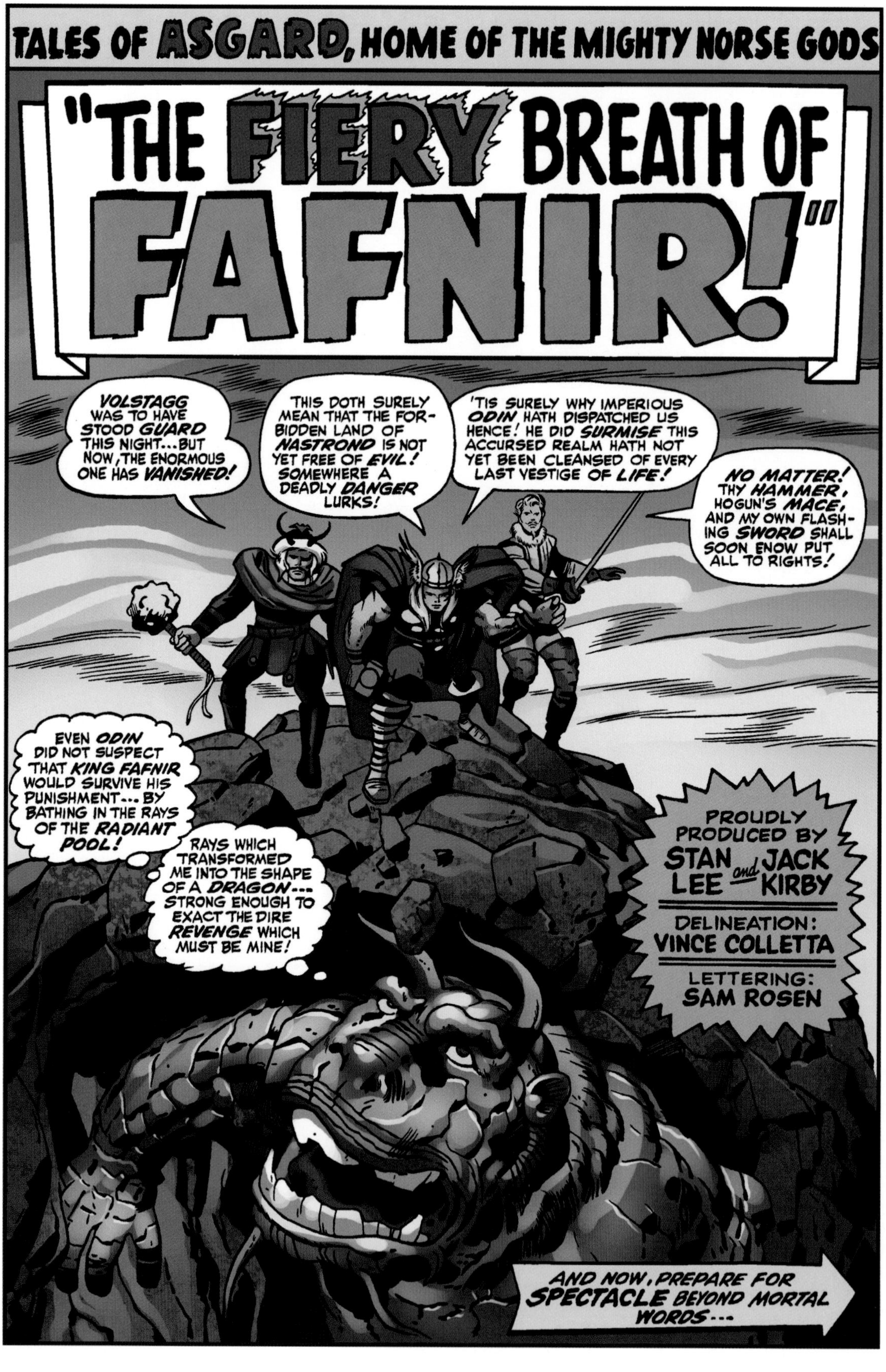
TALES OF ASGARD, HOME OF THE MIGHTY NORSE GODS
"THE FIERY BREATH OF FAFNIR!"
VOLSTAGG WAS TO HAVE STOOD GUARD THIS NIGHT...BUT NOW, THE ENORMOUS ONE HAS VANISHED!
THIS DOTH SURELY MEAN THAT THE FORBIDDEN LAND OF NASTROND IS NOT YET FREE OF EVIL! SOMEWHERE A DEADLY DANGER LURKS!
'TIS SURELY WHY IMPERIOUS ODIN HATH DISPATCHED US HENCE! HE DID SURMISE THIS ACCURSED REALM HATH NOT YET BEEN CLEANSED OF EVERY LAST VESTIGE OF LIFE!
NO MATTER! THY HAMMER, HOGUN'S MACE, AND MY OWN FLASHING SWORD SHALL SOON ENOW PUT ALL TO RIGHTS!
EVEN ODIN DID NOT SUSPECT THAT KING FAFNIR WOULD SURVIVE HIS PUNISHMENT... BY BATHING IN THE RAYS OF THE RADIANT POOL!
RAYS WHICH TRANSFORMED ME INTO THE SHAPE OF A DRAGON--- STRONG ENOUGH TO EXACT THE DIRE REVENGE WHICH MUST BE MINE!
PROUDLY PRODUCED BY STAN LEE and JACK KIRBY
DELINEATION: VINCE COLLETTA
LETTERING: SAM ROSEN
AND NOW, PREPARE FOR SPECTACLE BEYOND MORTAL WORDS---

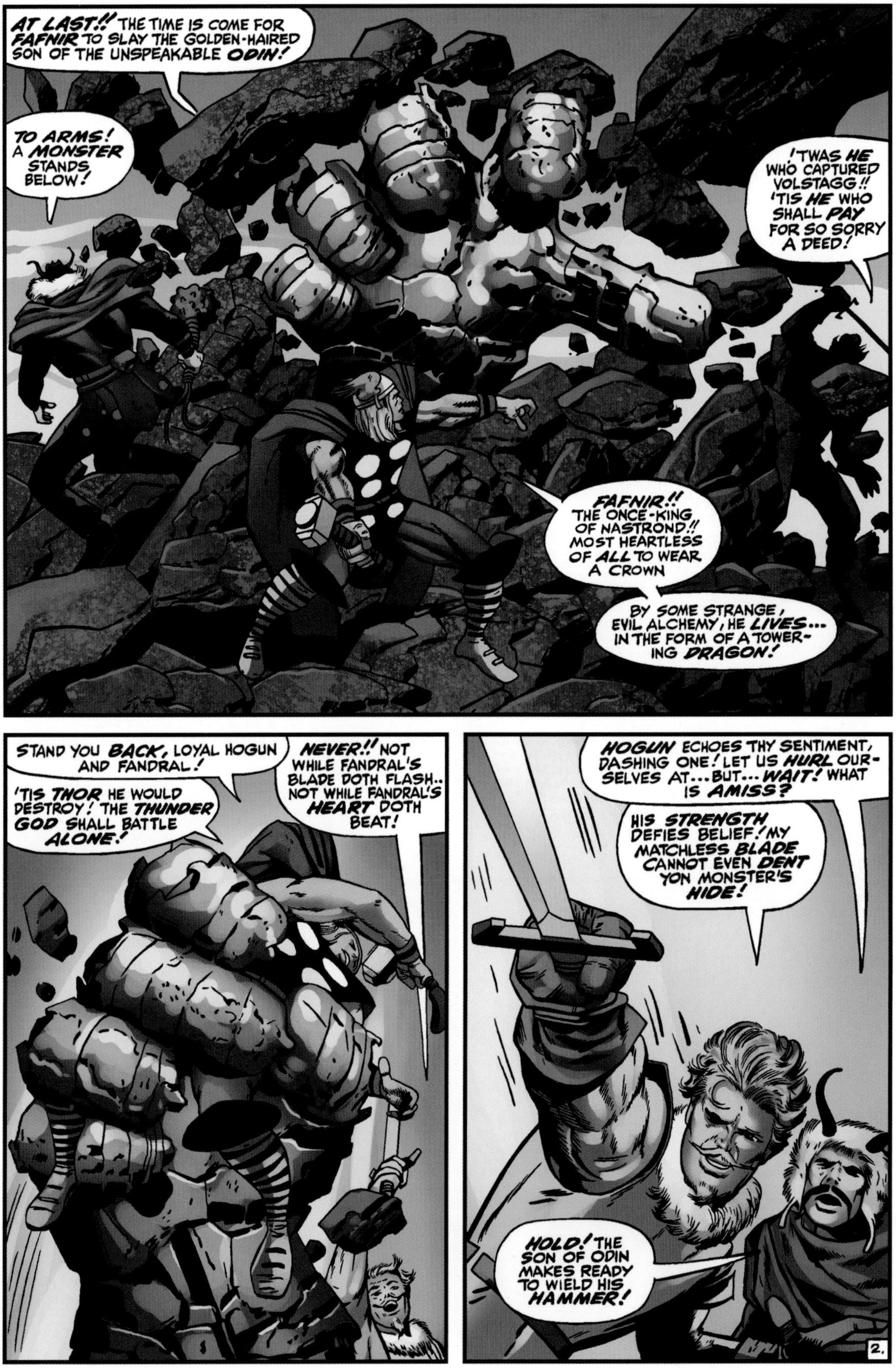
AT LAST!! THE TIME IS COME FOR FAFNIR TO SLAY THE GOLDEN-HAIRED SON OF THE UNSPEAKABLE ODIN!
TO ARMS! A MONSTER STANDS BELOW!
'TWAS HE WHO CAPTURED VOLSTAGG!! 'TIS HE WHO SHALL PAY FOR SO SORRY A DEED!
FAFNIR!! THE ONCE-KING OF NASTROND!! MOST HEARTLESS OF ALL TO WEAR A CROWN
BY SOME STRANGE, EVIL ALCHEMY, HE LIVES... IN THE FORM OF A TOWERING DRAGON!
STAND YOU BACK, LOYAL HOGUN AND FANDRAL!
'TIS THOR HE WOULD DESTROY! THE THUNDER GOD SHALL BATTLE ALONE!
NEVER!! NOT WHILE FANDRAL'S BLADE DOTH FLASH.. NOT WHILE FANDRAL'S HEART DOTH BEAT!
HOGUN ECHOES THY SENTIMENT, DASHING ONE! LET US HURL OURSELVES AT... BUT... WAIT! WHAT IS AMISS?
HIS STRENGTH DEFIES BELIEF! MY MATCHLESS BLADE CANNOT EVEN DENT YON MONSTER'S HIDE!
HOLD! THE SON OF ODIN MAKES READY TO WIELD HIS HAMMER!
2.

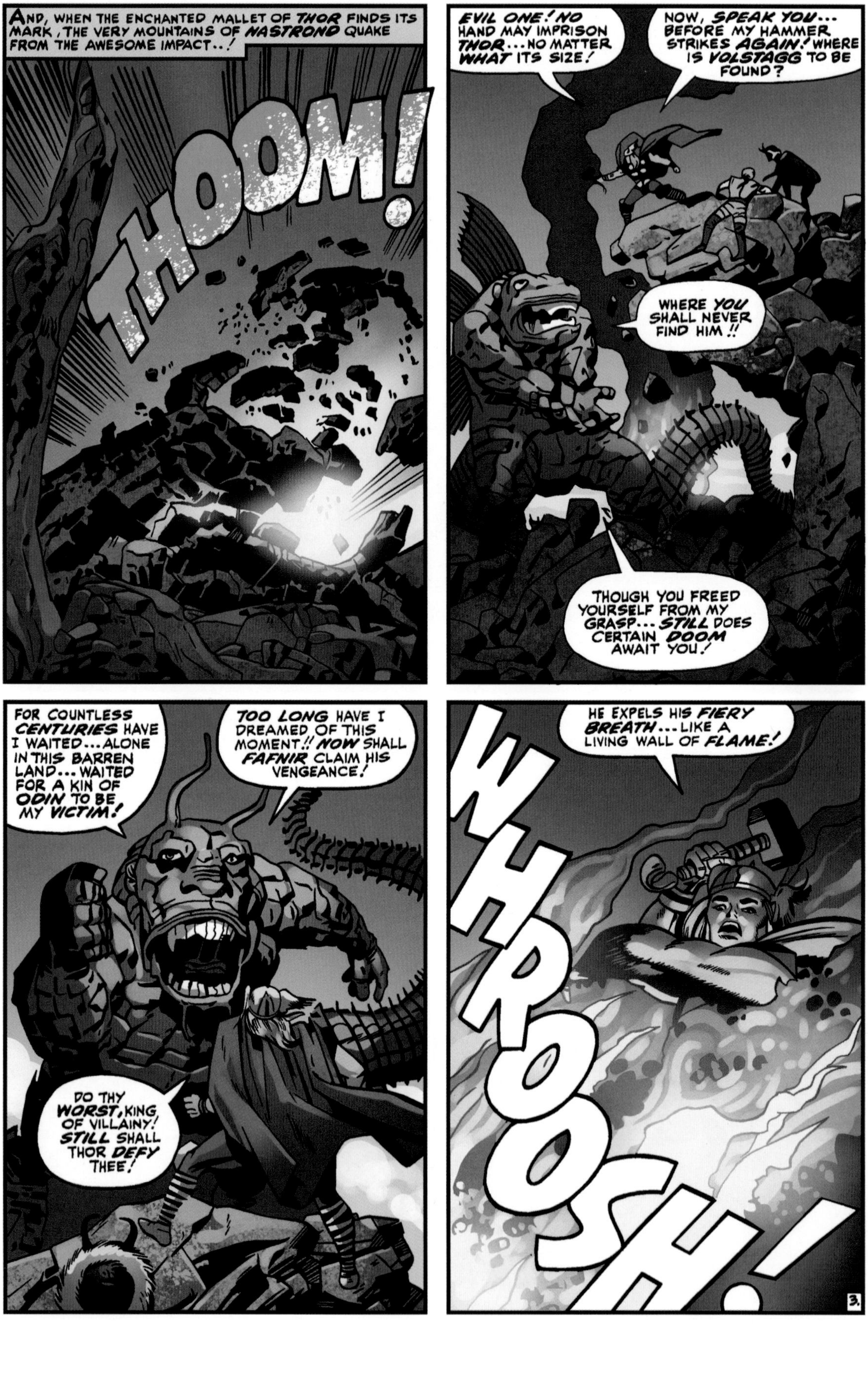
AND, WHEN THE ENCHANTED MALLET OF THOR FINDS ITS MARK, THE VERY MOUNTAINS OF NASTROND QUAKE FROM THE AWESOME IMPACT..!
THOOM!
EVIL ONE! NO HAND MAY IMPRISON THOR... NO MATTER WHAT ITS SIZE!
NOW, SPEAK YOU... BEFORE MY HAMMER STRIKES AGAIN! WHERE IS VOLSTAGG TO BE FOUND?
WHERE YOU SHALL NEVER FIND HIM!!
THOUGH YOU FREED YOURSELF FROM MY GRASP... STILL DOES CERTAIN DOOM AWAIT YOU!
FOR COUNTLESS CENTURIES HAVE I WAITED... ALONE IN THIS BARREN LAND... WAITED FOR A KIN OF ODIN TO BE MY VICTIM!
TOO LONG HAVE I DREAMED OF THIS MOMENT!! NOW SHALL FAFNIR CLAIM HIS VENGEANCE!
DO THY WORST, KING OF VILLAINY! STILL SHALL THOR DEFY THEE!
HE EXPELS HIS FIERY BREATH... LIKE A LIVING WALL OF FLAME!
WHROOSH!
3.

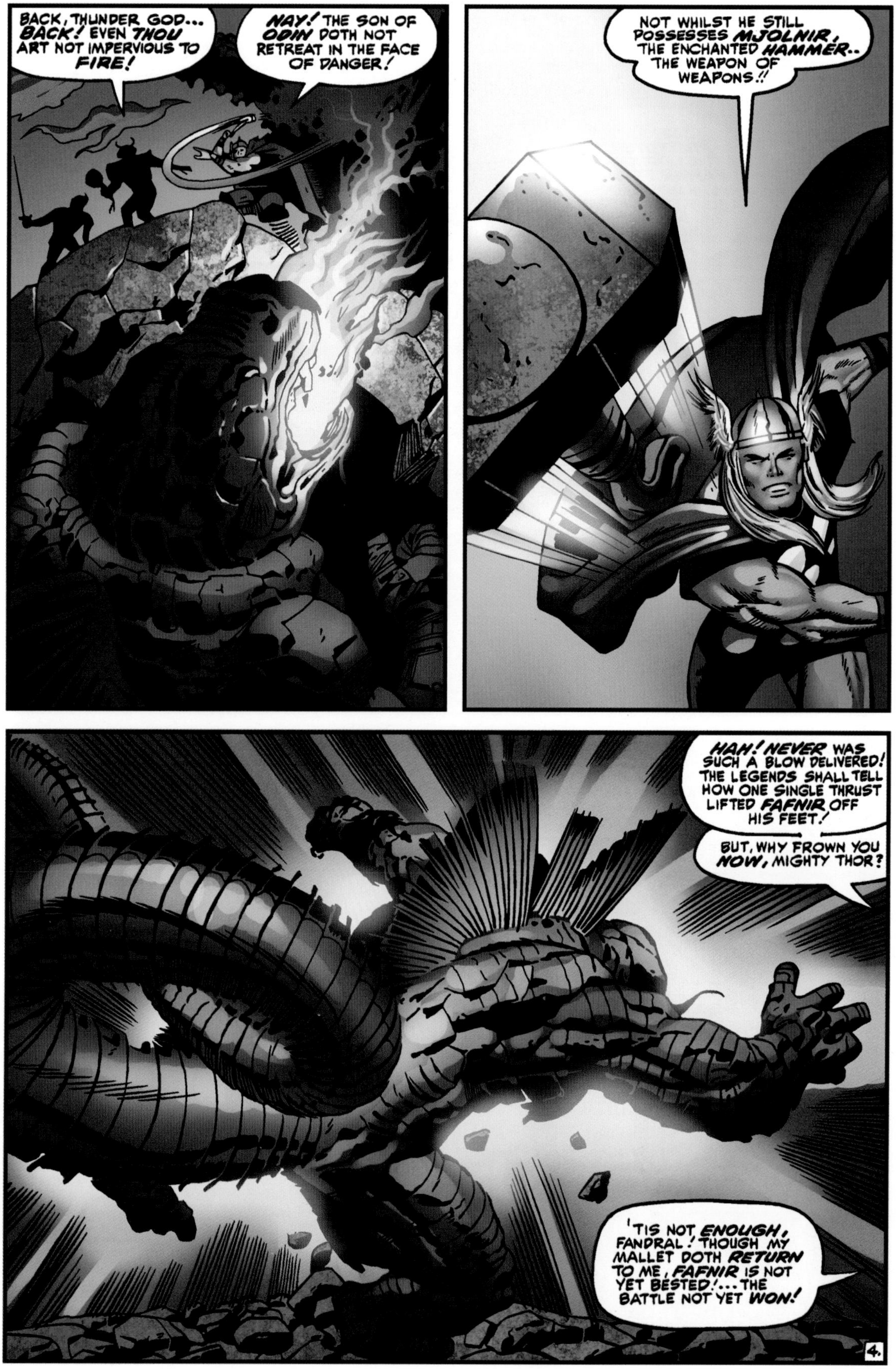
BACK, THUNDER GOD... BACK! EVEN THOU ART NOT IMPERVIOUS TO FIRE!
NAY! THE SON OF ODIN DOTH NOT RETREAT IN THE FACE OF DANGER!
NOT WHILST HE STILL POSSESSES MJOLNIR, THE ENCHANTED HAMMER.. THE WEAPON OF WEAPONS!!
HAH! NEVER WAS SUCH A BLOW DELIVERED! THE LEGENDS SHALL TELL HOW ONE SINGLE THRUST LIFTED FAFNIR OFF HIS FEET!
BUT, WHY FROWN YOU NOW, MIGHTY THOR?
'TIS NOT ENOUGH, FANDRAL! THOUGH MY MALLET DOTH RETURN TO ME, FAFNIR IS NOT YET BESTED!... THE BATTLE NOT YET WON!
4.

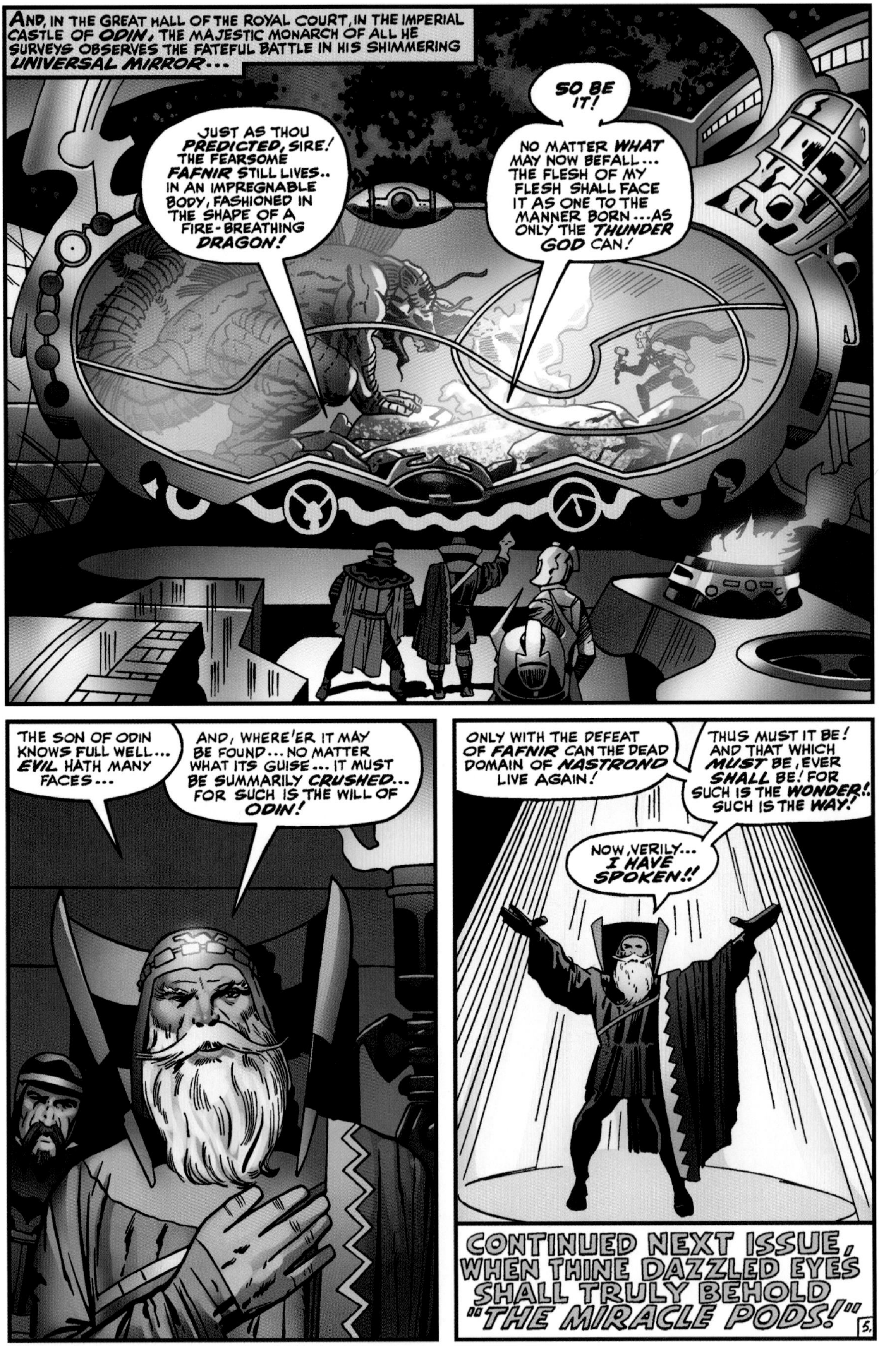
AND, IN THE GREAT HALL OF THE ROYAL COURT, IN THE IMPERIAL CASTLE OF ODIN, THE MAJESTIC MONARCH OF ALL HE SURVEYS OBSERVES THE FATEFUL BATTLE IN HIS SHIMMERING UNIVERSAL MIRROR...
JUST AS THOU PREDICTED, SIRE! THE FEARSOME FAFNIR STILL LIVES.. IN AN IMPREGNABLE BODY, FASHIONED IN THE SHAPE OF A FIRE-BREATHING DRAGON!
SO BE IT!
NO MATTER WHAT MAY NOW BEFALL... THE FLESH OF MY FLESH SHALL FACE IT AS ONE TO THE MANNER BORN...AS ONLY THE THUNDER GOD CAN!
THE SON OF ODIN KNOWS FULL WELL... EVIL HATH MANY FACES...
AND, WHERE'ER IT MAY BE FOUND... NO MATTER WHAT ITS GUISE... IT MUST BE SUMMARILY CRUSHED... FOR SUCH IS THE WILL OF ODIN!
ONLY WITH THE DEFEAT OF FAFNIR CAN THE DEAD DOMAIN OF NASTROND LIVE AGAIN!
THUS MUST IT BE! AND THAT WHICH MUST BE, EVER SHALL BE! FOR SUCH IS THE WONDER!.. SUCH IS THE WAY!
NOW, VERILY... I HAVE SPOKEN!!
CONTINUED NEXT ISSUE, WHEN THINE DAZZLED EYES SHALL TRULY BEHOLD "THE MIRACLE PODS!"
5.

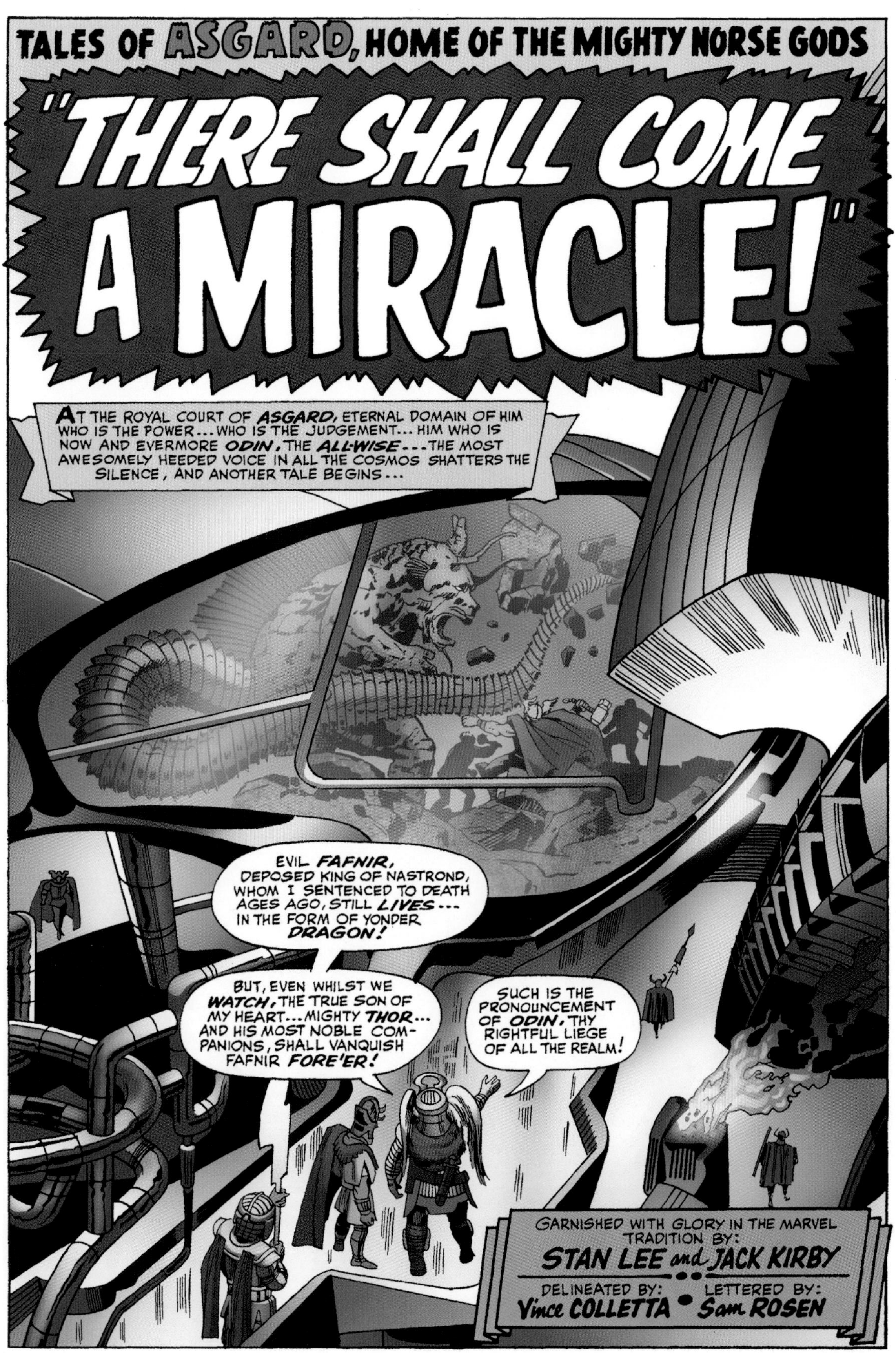
TALES OF ASGARD, HOME OF THE MIGHTY NORSE GODS
"THERE SHALL COME A MIRACLE!"
AT THE ROYAL COURT OF ASGARD, ETERNAL DOMAIN OF HIM WHO IS THE POWER... WHO IS THE JUDGEMENT... HIM WHO IS NOW AND EVERMORE ODIN, THE ALL-WISE... THE MOST AWESOMELY HEEDED VOICE IN ALL THE COSMOS SHATTERS THE SILENCE, AND ANOTHER TALE BEGINS...
EVIL FAFNIR, DEPOSED KING OF NASTROND, WHOM I SENTENCED TO DEATH AGES AGO, STILL LIVES... IN THE FORM OF YONDER DRAGON!
BUT, EVEN WHILST WE WATCH, THE TRUE SON OF MY HEART... MIGHTY THOR... AND HIS MOST NOBLE COMPANIONS, SHALL VANQUISH FAFNIR FORE'ER!
SUCH IS THE PRONOUNCEMENT OF ODIN, THY RIGHTFUL LIEGE OF ALL THE REALM!
GARNISHED WITH GLORY IN THE MARVEL TRADITION BY: STAN LEE and JACK KIRBY
DELINEATED BY: Vince COLLETTA • LETTERED BY: Sam ROSEN

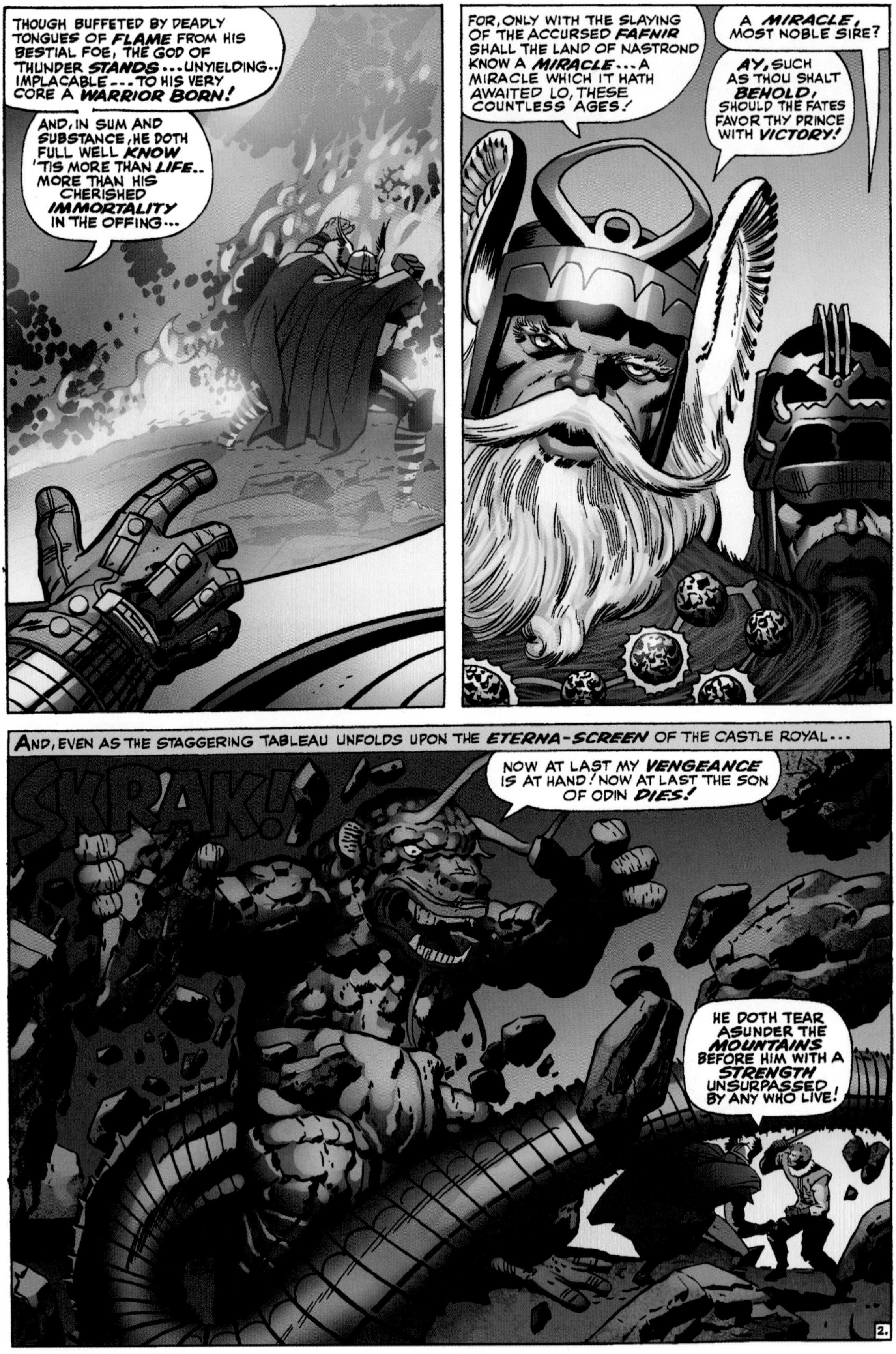
THOUGH BUFFETED BY DEADLY TONGUES OF FLAME FROM HIS BESTIAL FOE, THE GOD OF THUNDER STANDS... UNYIELDING.. IMPLACABLE... TO HIS VERY CORE A WARRIOR BORN!
AND, IN SUM AND SUBSTANCE, HE DOTH FULL WELL KNOW 'TIS MORE THAN LIFE.. MORE THAN HIS CHERISHED IMMORTALITY IN THE OFFING...
FOR, ONLY WITH THE SLAYING OF THE ACCURSED FAFNIR SHALL THE LAND OF NASTROND KNOW A MIRACLE... A MIRACLE WHICH IT HATH AWAITED LO, THESE COUNTLESS AGES!
A MIRACLE, MOST NOBLE SIRE?
AY, SUCH AS THOU SHALT BEHOLD, SHOULD THE FATES FAVOR THY PRINCE WITH VICTORY!
AND, EVEN AS THE STAGGERING TABLEAU UNFOLDS UPON THE ETERNA-SCREEN OF THE CASTLE ROYAL...
SKRAK!
NOW AT LAST MY VENGEANCE IS AT HAND! NOW AT LAST THE SON OF ODIN DIES!
HE DOTH TEAR ASUNDER THE MOUNTAINS BEFORE HIM WITH A STRENGTH UNSURPASSED BY ANY WHO LIVE!
2.

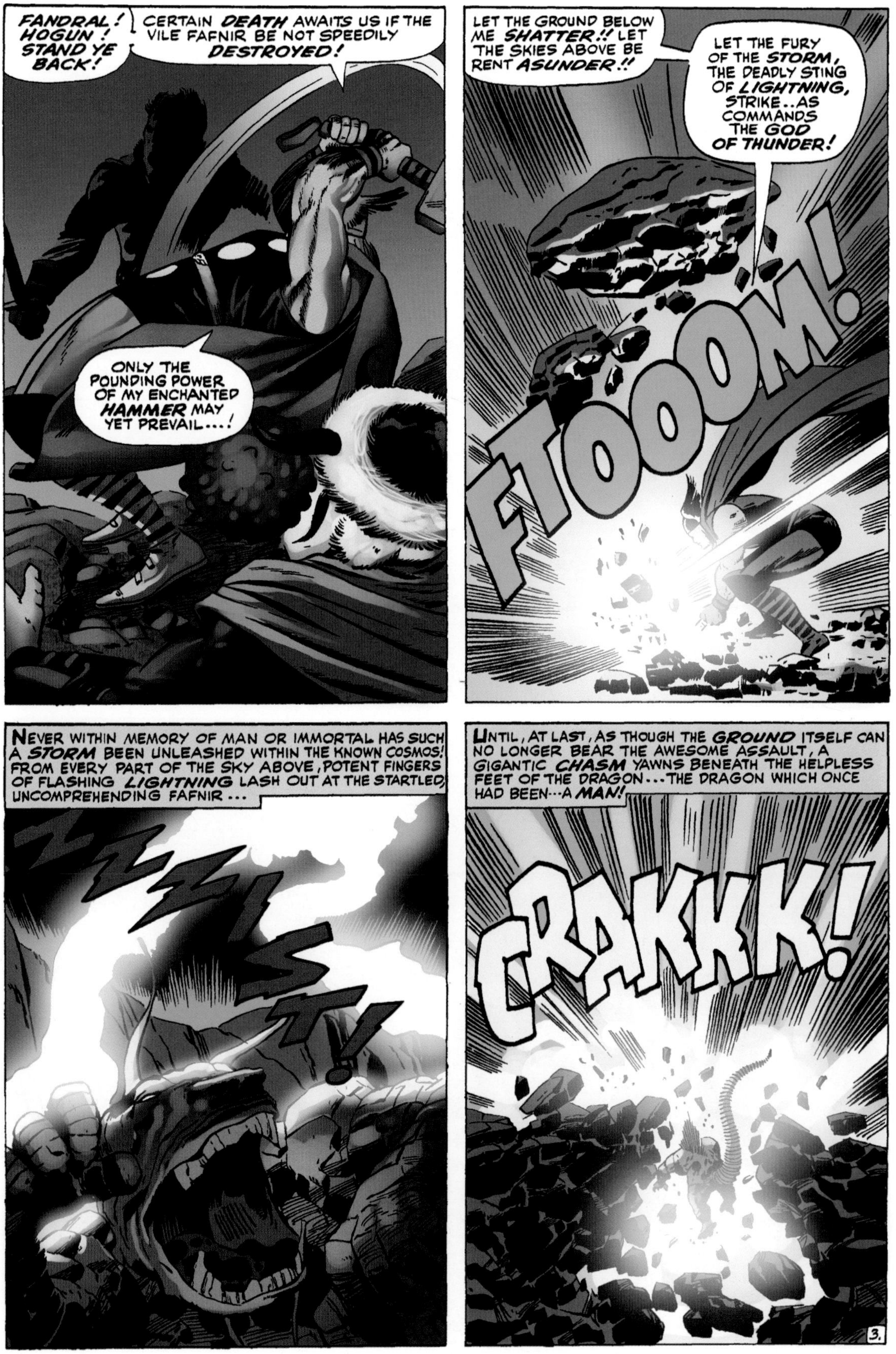
FANDRAL! HOGUN! STAND YE BACK!
CERTAIN DEATH AWAITS US IF THE VILE FAFNIR BE NOT SPEEDILY DESTROYED!
ONLY THE POUNDING POWER OF MY ENCHANTED HAMMER MAY YET PREVAIL...!
LET THE GROUND BELOW ME SHATTER!! LET THE SKIES ABOVE BE RENT ASUNDER!!
LET THE FURY OF THE STORM, THE DEADLY STING OF LIGHTNING, STRIKE..AS COMMANDS THE GOD OF THUNDER!
FTOOOM!
NEVER WITHIN MEMORY OF MAN OR IMMORTAL HAS SUCH A STORM BEEN UNLEASHED WITHIN THE KNOWN COSMOS! FROM EVERY PART OF THE SKY ABOVE, POTENT FINGERS OF FLASHING LIGHTNING LASH OUT AT THE STARTLED, UNCOMPREHENDING FAFNIR...
ZZZISST!
UNTIL, AT LAST, AS THOUGH THE GROUND ITSELF CAN NO LONGER BEAR THE AWESOME ASSAULT, A GIGANTIC CHASM YAWNS BENEATH THE HELPLESS FEET OF THE DRAGON... THE DRAGON WHICH ONCE HAD BEEN...A MAN!
CRAKKK!
3.

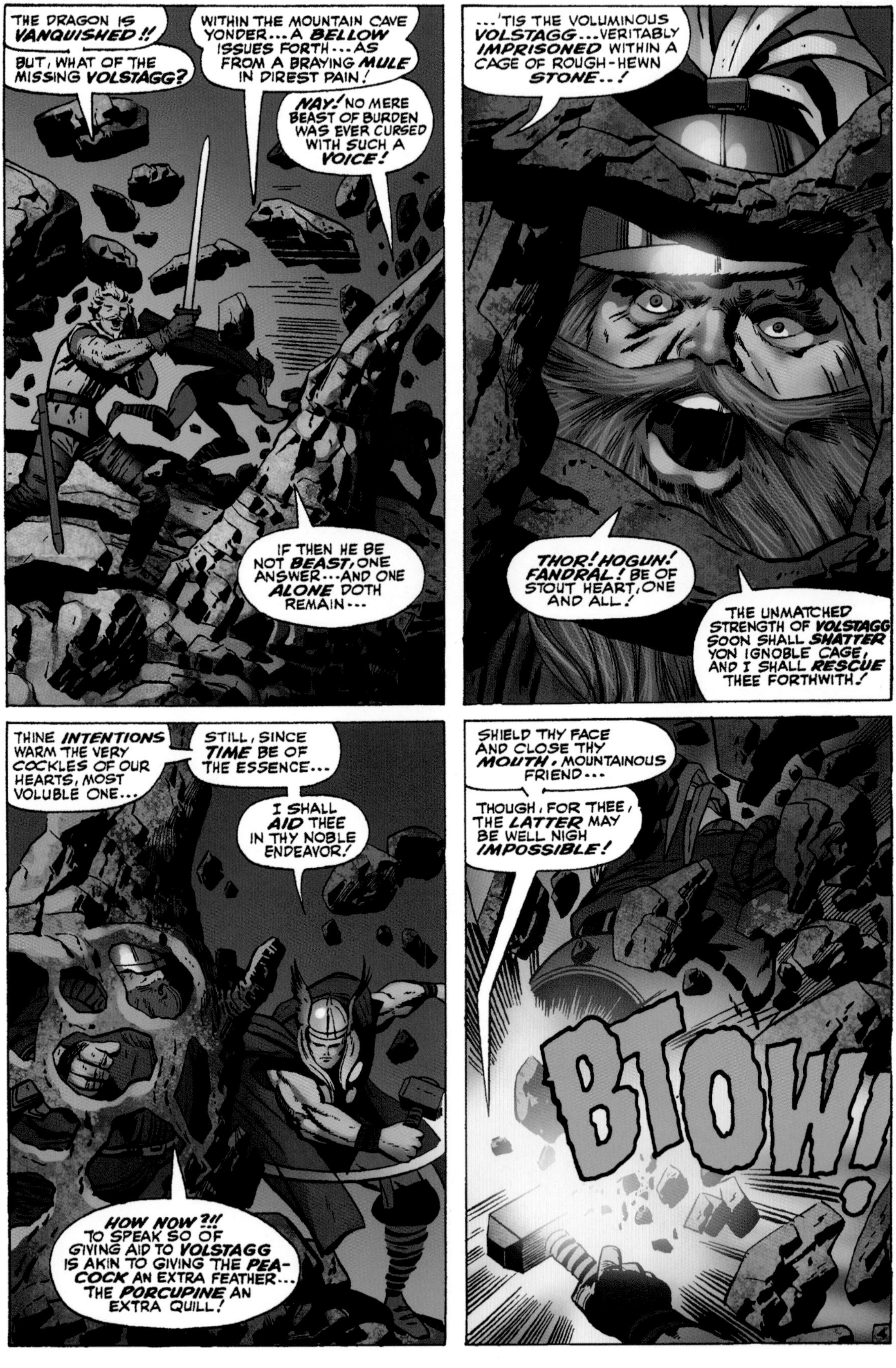
THE DRAGON IS VANQUISHED!!
BUT, WHAT OF THE MISSING VOLSTAGG?
WITHIN THE MOUNTAIN CAVE YONDER...A BELLOW ISSUES FORTH...AS FROM A BRAYING MULE IN DIREST PAIN!
NAY! NO MERE BEAST OF BURDEN WAS EVER CURSED WITH SUCH A VOICE!
IF THEN HE BE NOT BEAST, ONE ANSWER...AND ONE ALONE DOTH REMAIN...
...'TIS THE VOLUMINOUS VOLSTAGG...VERITABLY IMPRISONED WITHIN A CAGE OF ROUGH-HEWN STONE...!
THOR! HOGUN! FANDRAL! BE OF STOUT HEART, ONE AND ALL!
THE UNMATCHED STRENGTH OF VOLSTAGG SOON SHALL SHATTER YON IGNOBLE CAGE, AND I SHALL RESCUE THEE FORTHWITH!
THINE INTENTIONS WARM THE VERY COCKLES OF OUR HEARTS, MOST VOLUBLE ONE...
STILL, SINCE TIME BE OF THE ESSENCE...
I SHALL AID THEE IN THY NOBLE ENDEAVOR!
HOW NOW?!! TO SPEAK SO OF GIVING AID TO VOLSTAGG IS AKIN TO GIVING THE PEA-COCK AN EXTRA FEATHER...THE PORCUPINE AN EXTRA QUILL!
SHIELD THY FACE AND CLOSE THY MOUTH, MOUNTAINOUS FRIEND...
THOUGH, FOR THEE, THE LATTER MAY BE WELL NIGH IMPOSSIBLE!
BTOW

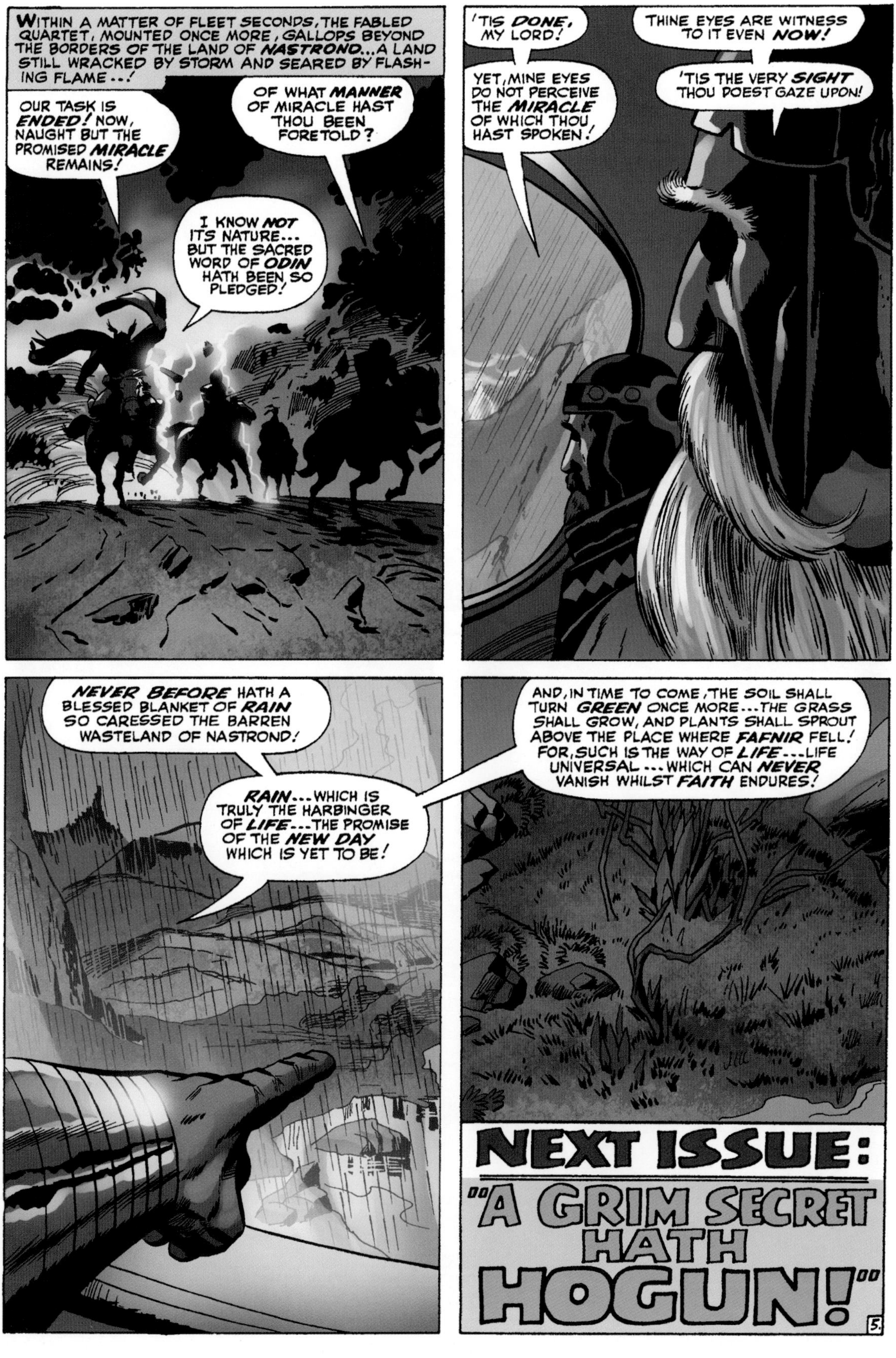
WITHIN A MATTER OF FLEET SECONDS, THE FABLED QUARTET, MOUNTED ONCE MORE, GALLOPS BEYOND THE BORDERS OF THE LAND OF NASTROND... A LAND STILL WRACKED BY STORM AND SEARED BY FLASHING FLAME...!
OUR TASK IS ENDED! NOW, NAUGHT BUT THE PROMISED MIRACLE REMAINS!
OF WHAT MANNER OF MIRACLE HAST THOU BEEN FORETOLD?
I KNOW NOT ITS NATURE... BUT THE SACRED WORD OF ODIN HATH BEEN SO PLEDGED!
'TIS DONE, MY LORD!
THINE EYES ARE WITNESS TO IT EVEN NOW!
YET, MINE EYES DO NOT PERCEIVE THE MIRACLE OF WHICH THOU HAST SPOKEN!
'TIS THE VERY SIGHT THOU DOEST GAZE UPON!
NEVER BEFORE HATH A BLESSED BLANKET OF RAIN SO CARESSED THE BARREN WASTELAND OF NASTROND!
RAIN... WHICH IS TRULY THE HARBINGER OF LIFE... THE PROMISE OF THE NEW DAY WHICH IS YET TO BE!
AND, IN TIME TO COME, THE SOIL SHALL TURN GREEN ONCE MORE... THE GRASS SHALL GROW, AND PLANTS SHALL SPROUT ABOVE THE PLACE WHERE FAFNIR FELL! FOR, SUCH IS THE WAY OF LIFE... LIFE UNIVERSAL... WHICH CAN NEVER VANISH WHILST FAITH ENDURES!
NEXT ISSUE:
"A GRIM SECRET HATH HOGUN!"
5.

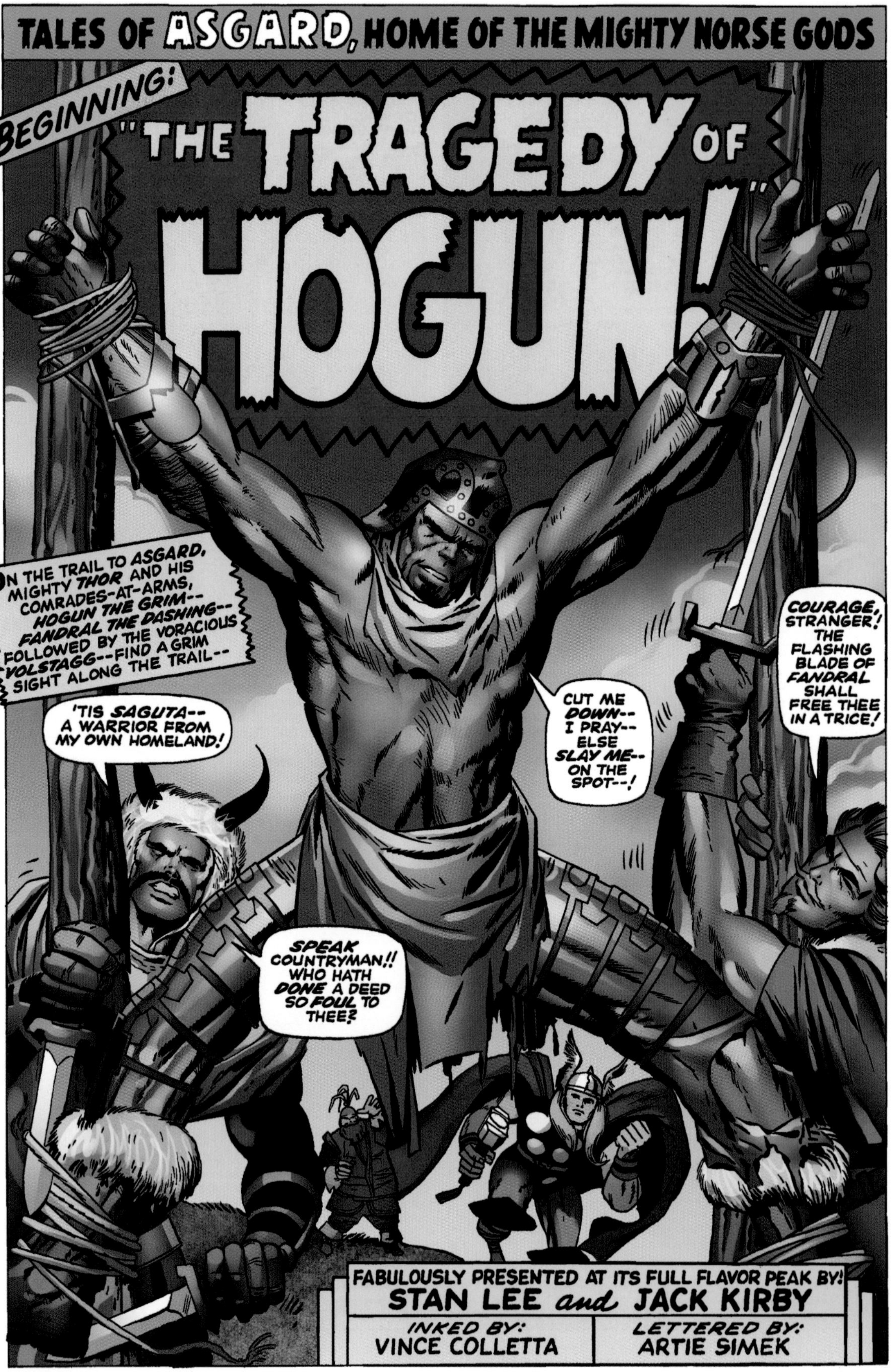
TALES OF ASGARD, HOME OF THE MIGHTY NORSE GODS
BEGINNING:
"THE TRAGEDY OF HOGUN!"
ON THE TRAIL TO ASGARD, MIGHTY THOR AND HIS COMRADES-AT-ARMS, HOGUN THE GRIM-- FANDRAL THE DASHING-- FOLLOWED BY THE VORACIOUS VOLSTAGG--FIND A GRIM SIGHT ALONG THE TRAIL--
'TIS SAGUTA-- A WARRIOR FROM MY OWN HOMELAND!
CUT ME DOWN-- I PRAY-- ELSE SLAY ME-- ON THE SPOT--!
COURAGE, STRANGER! THE FLASHING BLADE OF FANDRAL SHALL FREE THEE IN A TRICE!
SPEAK COUNTRYMAN!! WHO HATH DONE A DEED SO FOUL TO THEE?
FABULOUSLY PRESENTED AT ITS FULL FLAVOR PEAK BY! STAN LEE and JACK KIRBY
INKED BY: VINCE COLLETTA
LETTERED BY: ARTIE SIMEK

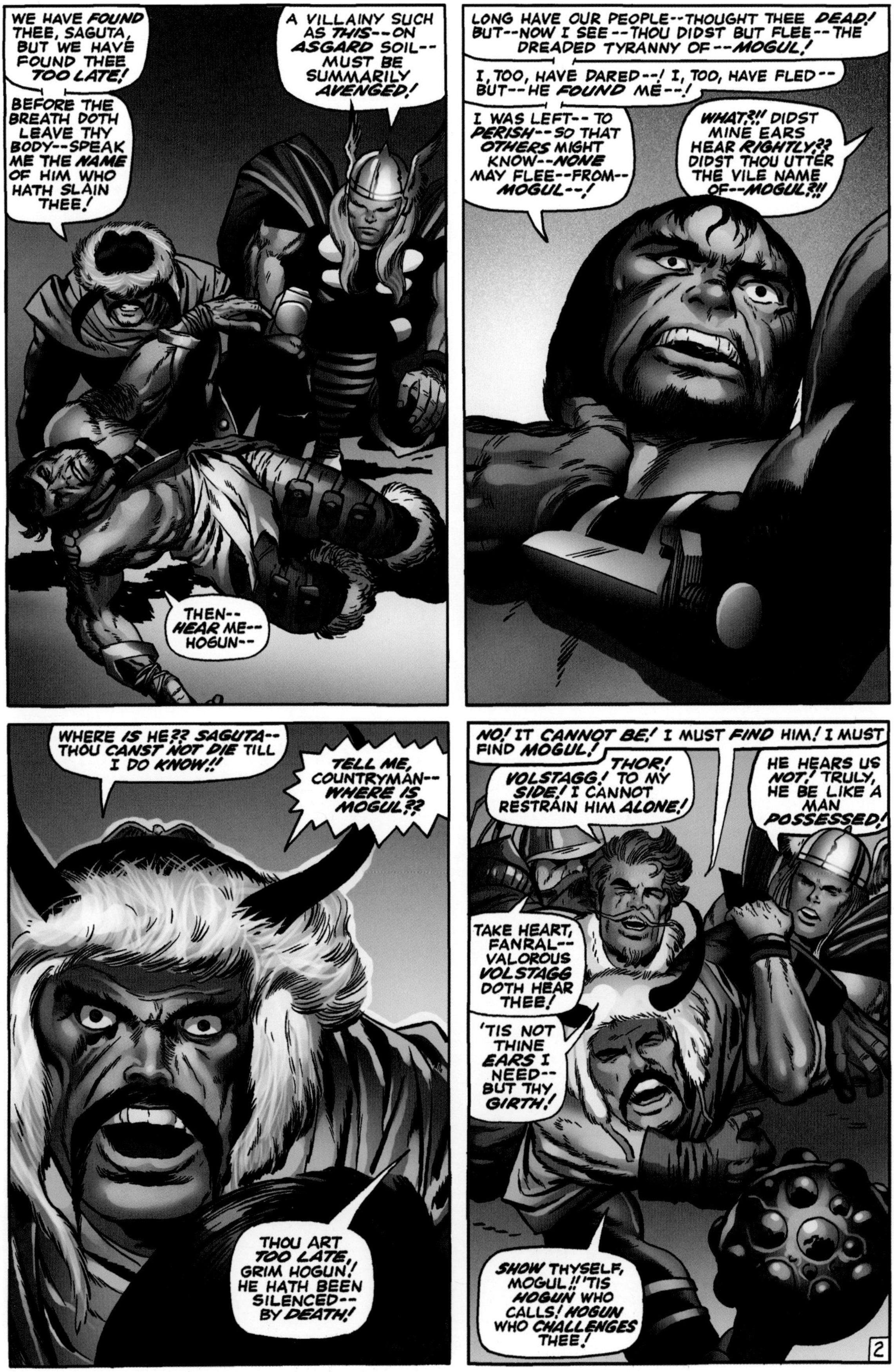
WE HAVE FOUND THEE, SAGUTA, BUT WE HAVE FOUND THEE TOO LATE!
BEFORE THE BREATH DOTH LEAVE THY BODY--SPEAK ME THE NAME OF HIM WHO HATH SLAIN THEE!
A VILLAINY SUCH AS THIS--ON ASGARD SOIL--MUST BE SUMMARILY AVENGED!
THEN--HEAR ME--HOGUN--
LONG HAVE OUR PEOPLE--THOUGHT THEE DEAD! BUT--NOW I SEE--THOU DIDST BUT FLEE--THE DREADED TYRANNY OF--MOGUL!
I, TOO, HAVE DARED--! I, TOO, HAVE FLED--BUT--HE FOUND ME--!
I WAS LEFT--TO PERISH--SO THAT OTHERS MIGHT KNOW--NONE MAY FLEE--FROM--MOGUL--!
WHAT?!! DIDST MINE EARS HEAR RIGHTLY?? DIDST THOU UTTER THE VILE NAME OF--MOGUL?!!
WHERE IS HE?? SAGUTA--THOU CANST NOT DIE TILL I DO KNOW!!
TELL ME, COUNTRYMAN--WHERE IS MOGUL??
THOU ART TOO LATE, GRIM HOGUN! HE HATH BEEN SILENCED--BY DEATH!
NO! IT CANNOT BE! I MUST FIND HIM! I MUST FIND MOGUL!
THOR! VOLSTAGG! TO MY SIDE! I CANNOT RESTRAIN HIM ALONE!
HE HEARS US NOT! TRULY, HE BE LIKE A MAN POSSESSED!
TAKE HEART, FANRAL--VALOROUS VOLSTAGG DOTH HEAR THEE!
'TIS NOT THINE EARS I NEED--BUT THY GIRTH!
SHOW THYSELF, MOGUL!! 'TIS HOGUN WHO CALLS! HOGUN WHO CHALLENGES THEE!
2

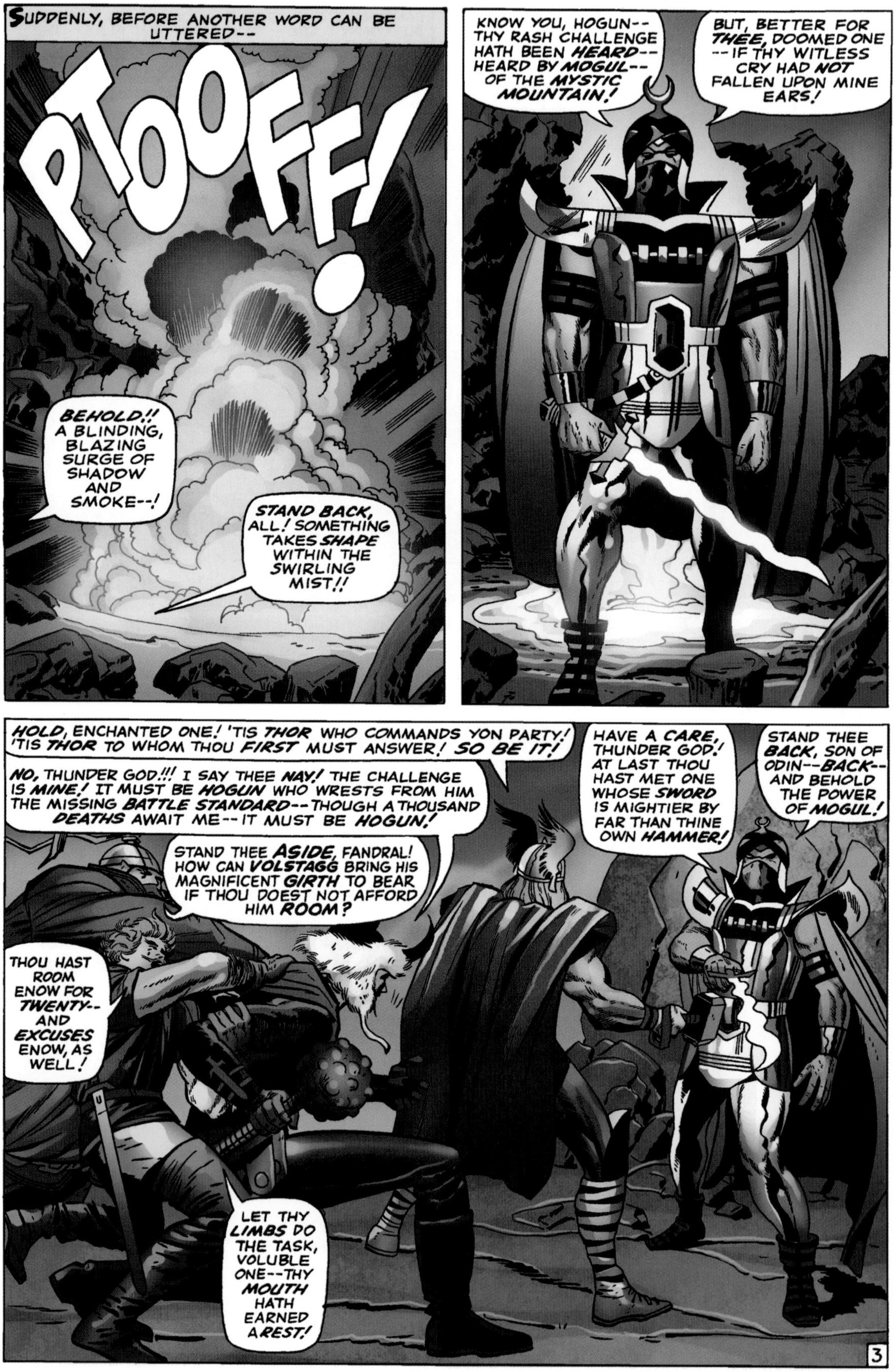
SUDDENLY, BEFORE ANOTHER WORD CAN BE UTTERED--
PTOOFF!
BEHOLD!! A BLINDING, BLAZING SURGE OF SHADOW AND SMOKE--!
STAND BACK, ALL! SOMETHING TAKES SHAPE WITHIN THE SWIRLING MIST!!
KNOW YOU, HOGUN-- THY RASH CHALLENGE HATH BEEN HEARD-- HEARD BY MOGUL-- OF THE MYSTIC MOUNTAIN!
BUT, BETTER FOR THEE, DOOMED ONE --IF THY WITLESS CRY HAD NOT FALLEN UPON MINE EARS!
HOLD, ENCHANTED ONE! 'TIS THOR WHO COMMANDS YON PARTY! 'TIS THOR TO WHOM THOU FIRST MUST ANSWER! SO BE IT!
NO, THUNDER GOD!!! I SAY THEE NAY! THE CHALLENGE IS MINE! IT MUST BE HOGUN WHO WRESTS FROM HIM THE MISSING BATTLE STANDARD--THOUGH A THOUSAND DEATHS AWAIT ME--IT MUST BE HOGUN!
HAVE A CARE, THUNDER GOD! AT LAST THOU HAST MET ONE WHOSE SWORD IS MIGHTIER BY FAR THAN THINE OWN HAMMER!
STAND THEE BACK, SON OF ODIN--BACK-- AND BEHOLD THE POWER OF MOGUL!
STAND THEE ASIDE, FANDRAL! HOW CAN VOLSTAGG BRING HIS MAGNIFICENT GIRTH TO BEAR IF THOU DOEST NOT AFFORD HIM ROOM?
THOU HAST ROOM ENOW FOR TWENTY-- AND EXCUSES ENOW, AS WELL!
LET THY LIMBS DO THE TASK, VOLUBLE ONE--THY MOUTH HATH EARNED A REST!
3

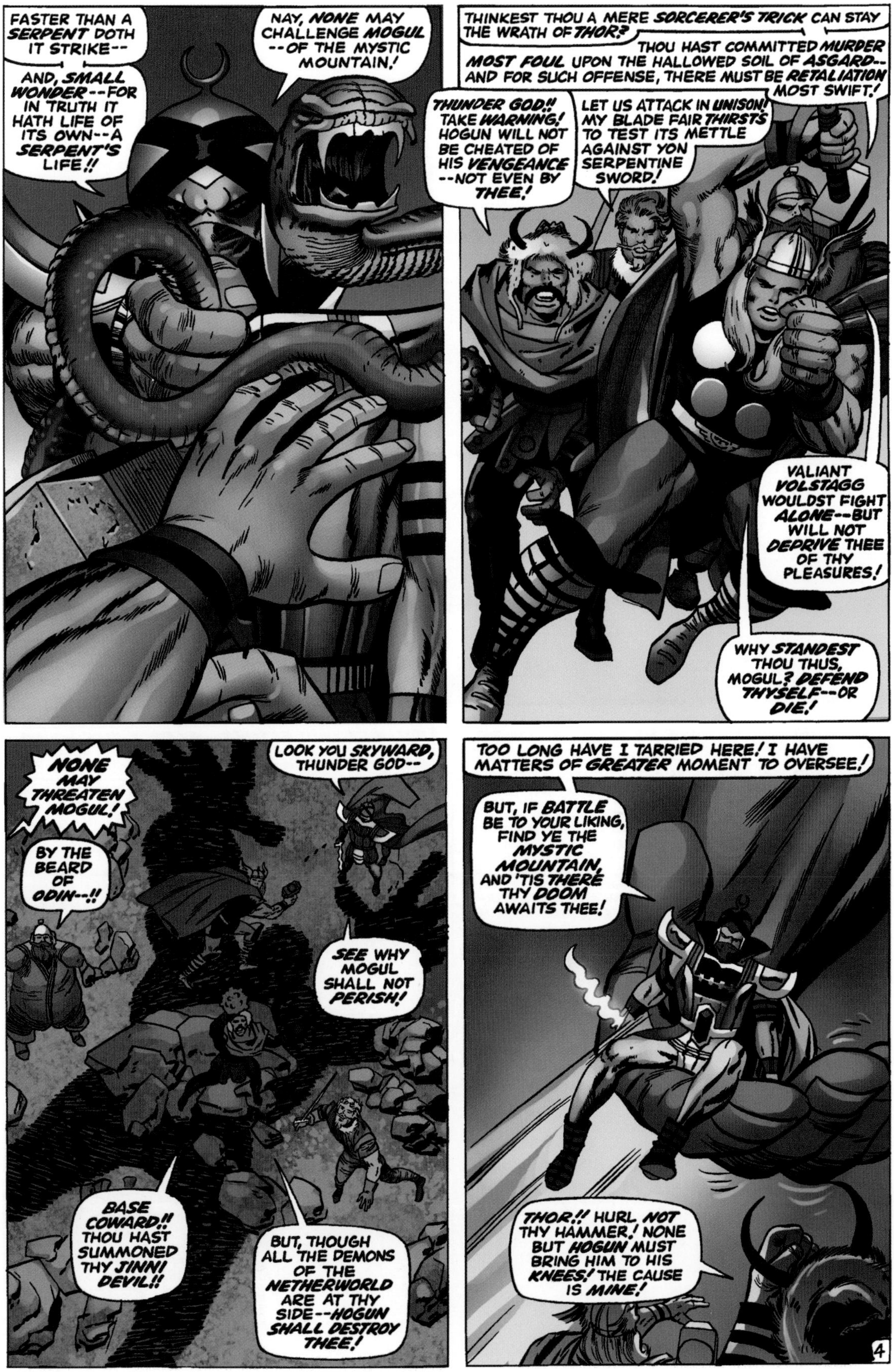
FASTER THAN A SERPENT DOTH IT STRIKE--
AND, SMALL WONDER--FOR IN TRUTH IT HATH LIFE OF ITS OWN--A SERPENT'S LIFE!!
NAY, NONE MAY CHALLENGE MOGUL--OF THE MYSTIC MOUNTAIN!
THINKEST THOU A MERE SORCERER'S TRICK CAN STAY THE WRATH OF THOR?
THOU HAST COMMITTED MURDER MOST FOUL UPON THE HALLOWED SOIL OF ASGARD--AND FOR SUCH OFFENSE, THERE MUST BE RETALIATION MOST SWIFT!
THUNDER GOD!! TAKE WARNING! HOGUN WILL NOT BE CHEATED OF HIS VENGEANCE--NOT EVEN BY THEE!
LET US ATTACK IN UNISON! MY BLADE FAIR THIRSTS TO TEST ITS METTLE AGAINST YON SERPENTINE SWORD!
VALIANT VOLSTAGG WOULDST FIGHT ALONE--BUT WILL NOT DEPRIVE THEE OF THY PLEASURES!
WHY STANDEST THOU THUS, MOGUL? DEFEND THYSELF--OR DIE!
NONE MAY THREATEN MOGUL!
BY THE BEARD OF ODIN--!!
LOOK YOU SKYWARD, THUNDER GOD--
SEE WHY MOGUL SHALL NOT PERISH!
BASE COWARD!! THOU HAST SUMMONED THY JINNI DEVIL!!
BUT, THOUGH ALL THE DEMONS OF THE NETHERWORLD ARE AT THY SIDE--HOGUN SHALL DESTROY THEE!
TOO LONG HAVE I TARRIED HERE! I HAVE MATTERS OF GREATER MOMENT TO OVERSEE!
BUT, IF BATTLE BE TO YOUR LIKING, FIND YE THE MYSTIC MOUNTAIN, AND 'TIS THERE THY DOOM AWAITS THEE!
THOR!! HURL NOT THY HAMMER! NONE BUT HOGUN MUST BRING HIM TO HIS KNEES! THE CAUSE IS MINE!
4

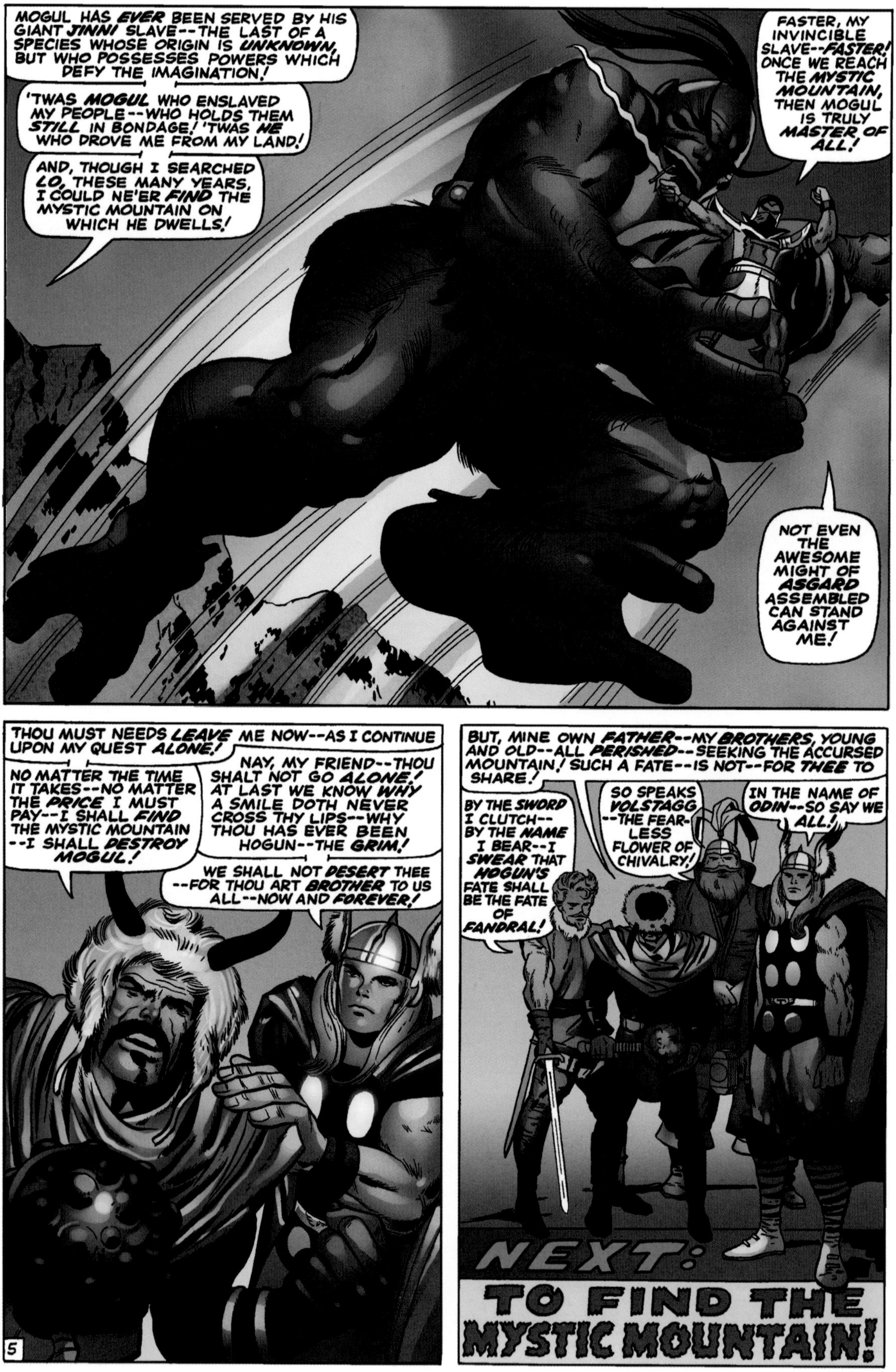
MOGUL HAS EVER BEEN SERVED BY HIS GIANT JINNI SLAVE--THE LAST OF A SPECIES WHOSE ORIGIN IS UNKNOWN, BUT WHO POSSESSES POWERS WHICH DEFY THE IMAGINATION!
'TWAS MOGUL WHO ENSLAVED MY PEOPLE--WHO HOLDS THEM STILL IN BONDAGE! 'TWAS HE WHO DROVE ME FROM MY LAND!
AND, THOUGH I SEARCHED LO, THESE MANY YEARS, I COULD NE'ER FIND THE MYSTIC MOUNTAIN ON WHICH HE DWELLS!
FASTER, MY INVINCIBLE SLAVE--FASTER! ONCE WE REACH THE MYSTIC MOUNTAIN, THEN MOGUL IS TRULY MASTER OF ALL!
NOT EVEN THE AWESOME MIGHT OF ASGARD ASSEMBLED CAN STAND AGAINST ME!
THOU MUST NEEDS LEAVE ME NOW--AS I CONTINUE UPON MY QUEST ALONE!
NO MATTER THE TIME IT TAKES--NO MATTER THE PRICE I MUST PAY--I SHALL FIND THE MYSTIC MOUNTAIN --I SHALL DESTROY MOGUL!
NAY, MY FRIEND--THOU SHALT NOT GO ALONE! AT LAST WE KNOW WHY A SMILE DOTH NEVER CROSS THY LIPS--WHY THOU HAS EVER BEEN HOGUN--THE GRIM!
WE SHALL NOT DESERT THEE --FOR THOU ART BROTHER TO US ALL--NOW AND FOREVER!
5
BUT, MINE OWN FATHER--MY BROTHERS, YOUNG AND OLD--ALL PERISHED--SEEKING THE ACCURSED MOUNTAIN! SUCH A FATE--IS NOT--FOR THEE TO SHARE!
BY THE SWORD I CLUTCH-- BY THE NAME I BEAR--I SWEAR THAT HOGUN'S FATE SHALL BE THE FATE OF FANDRAL!
SO SPEAKS VOLSTAGG --THE FEAR-LESS FLOWER OF CHIVALRY!
IN THE NAME OF ODIN--SO SAY WE ALL!
NEXT:
TO FIND THE MYSTIC MOUNTAIN!

WARRIORS THREE

The Warriors Three are three of Asgard's most celebrated heroes, Hogun, Fandral, and Volstagg, longtime friends who usually work together as a team (see *Asgard*). Their first known mission together took place at an unknown time in the past when they joined the quest by sea led by the prince of Asgard, Thor, to discover the reason why a crack had appeared in the Odinsword (also called Oversword) of Asgard, a power object that could bring about Asgard's destruction (see *Thor, Appendix: Odinsword*). Hogun, Fandral, and Volstagg aided Thor in quelling a mutiny led against Thor, on this mission by his adoptive brother Loki (see *Loki*). Since then Hogun, Fandral, and Volstagg have been Thor's friends, allies, and companions, and have aided him in numerous exploits.

Hogun the Grim is not a native of Asgard, but originally came from an unnamed land elsewhere in the Asgardian dimension. Hogun's homeland was conquered by Mogul of the Mystic Mountain, but together Thor and the Warriors Three defeated Mogul and liberated Hogun's homeland (see *Appendix: Mogul of the Mystic Mountain*).

In contrast with Hogun, who bears a somber demeanor, Fandral the Dashing is known for his humor, high spirits, and love of displaying his prowess with the sword in battle.

Volstagg is older than his two companions, and is rumored to have been one of Asgard's greatest warriors in his youth. Volstagg and his wife Gudrun are raising an enormous family, of whom the best-known member is their spirited daughter Gunnhild ("Hildy"). Recently Volstagg has adopted two children from Earth, Kevin and Mick, the orphaned sons of a woman named Ruby, who was killed by Thor's enemy, the Zaniac (see *Appendix: Zaniac*). Volstagg is motivated to join Hogun and Fandral in exploits both by a love of adventure and by a need to get away from his large family (whom he nonetheless deeply loves) from time to time. Although Volstagg's boastfulness about his battle prowess is sometimes belied by his occasional clumsiness, he remains a far more formidable opponent than his appearance would suggest.

Like other Asgardians, the Warriors Three are extremely long-lived (although not immortal like the Olympian gods), superhumanly strong, immune to all terrestrial diseases, resistant to conventional injury, and in possession of superhuman endurance (see *Asgardians*).

VOLSTAGG

Real name: Volstagg
Occupation: Warrior, father, adventurer
Identity: The general populace of Earth knows of Volstagg but does not acknowledge his godhood
Legal status: Citizen of Asgard
Other aliases: Volstagg the Enormous, the Lion of Asgard
Place of birth: Asgard
Marital status: Married
Known relatives: Gudrun (wife), Alaric, Rolfe (sons), Flosi, Gudrun, Gunnhild ("Hildy") (daughters), Kevin, Mick (adopted sons)
Base of operation: Asgard
First appearance: JOURNEY INTO MYSTERY #119
Height: 6' 8"
Weight: Unknown
Eyes: Blue
Hair: Red
Strength level: In his prime Volstagg could lift (press) about 40 tons. Now he can lift about 35.
Known superhuman powers: Volstagg possesses the conventional superhuman physical attributes of an Asgardian god.
Abilities: In his prime Volstagg is said to have been a great warrior. Although no longer as physically fit as he once was, Volstagg can still use his tremendous bulk to his advantage in combat.

HOGUN

Real name: Hogun
Occupation: Warrior
Identity: The general populace of Earth knows of Hogun but does not acknowledge his godhood
Legal status: Naturalized citizen of Asgard
Other aliases: Hogun the Grim
Place of birth: An unnamed land in the Asgardian dimension
Marital status: Single
Known relatives: None
Base of operation: Asgard
First appearance: JOURNEY INTO MYSTERY #119
Height: 6' 3"
Weight: 590 lbs.
Eyes: Grey blue
Hair: Black
Strength level: Hogun can lift (press) about 35 tons.
Abilities: Hogun is a superb hand-to-hand combatant and horseman.
Weapons: Hogun's preferred weapon is the mace.

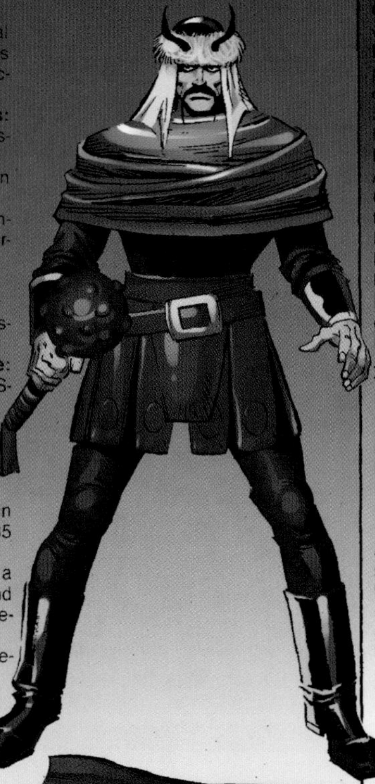

FANDRAL

Real name: Fandral
Occupation: Warrior adventurer
Identity: The general populace of Earth knows of Fandral but does not acknowledge his godhood
Legal status: Citizen of Asgard
Other aliases: Fandral the Dashing
Place of birth: Asgard
Marital status: Single
Known relatives: None
Base of operation: Asgard
First appearance: JOURNEY INTO MYSTERY #119
Height: 6' 4"
Weight: 585 lbs.
Eyes: Blue
Hair: Blond
Strength level: Fandral can lift (press) about 30 tons.
Abilities: Fandral is unsurpassed in Asgard in his mastery of swordsmanship. He is good hand-to-hand combatant and an excellent horseman.
Weapons: Fandral's preferred weapon is the sword.

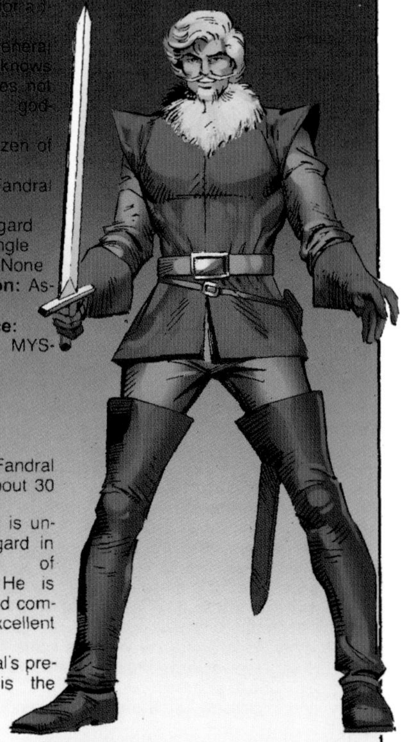

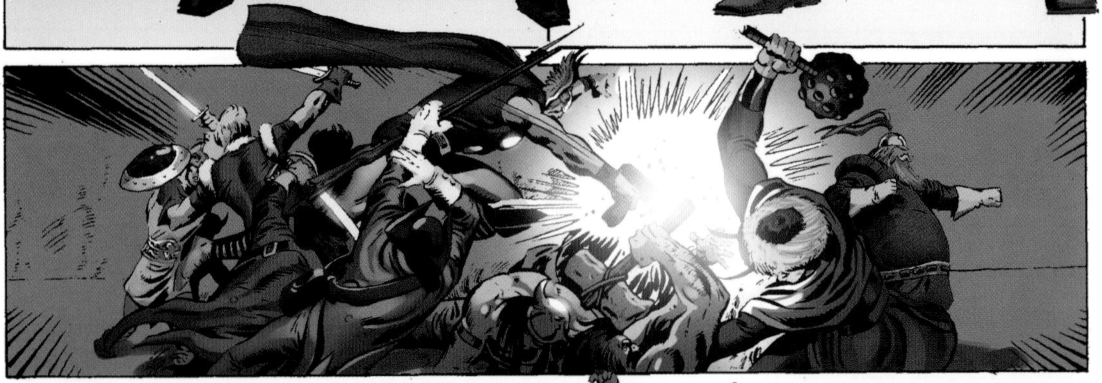

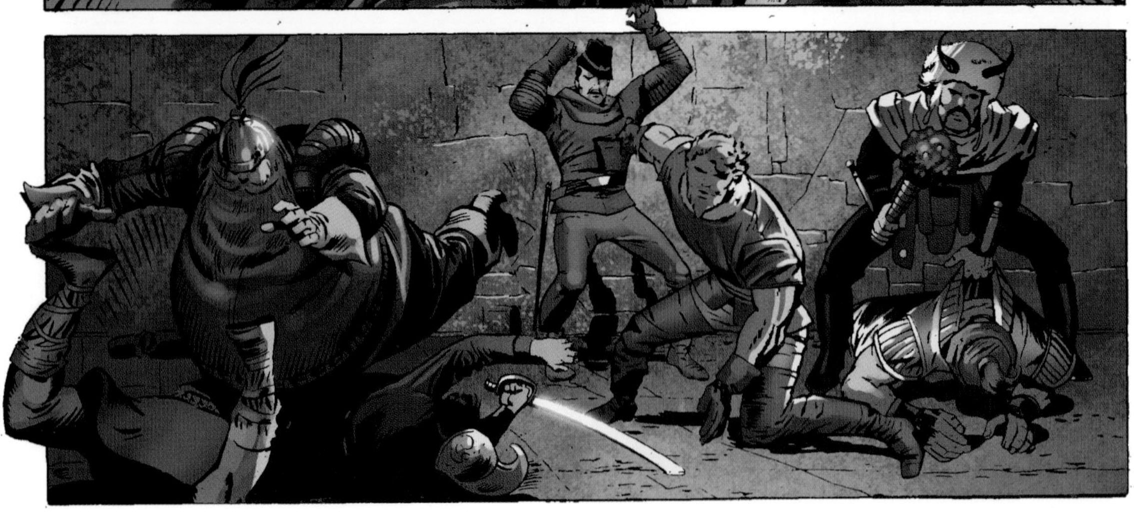